C000136797

THE DUCHESS TAKES A LOVER

Ladies of Seduction
Book One

Jillian Eaton

DRAGONBLADE PUBLISHING, INC.

© Copyright 2024 by Jillian Eaton
Text by Jillian Eaton
Cover by Dar Albert

Dragonblade Publishing, Inc. is an imprint of Kathryn Le Veque Novels, Inc.
P.O. Box 23
Moreno Valley, CA 92556
ceo@dragonbladepublishing.com

Produced in the United States of America

First Edition February 2024
Trade Paperback Edition

Reproduction of any kind except where it pertains to short quotes in relation to advertising or promotion is strictly prohibited.

All Rights Reserved.

The characters and events portrayed in this book are fictitious. Any similarity to real persons, living or dead, is purely coincidental and not intended by the author.

ARE YOU SIGNED UP FOR DRAGONBLADE'S BLOG?

You'll get the latest news and information on exclusive giveaways, exclusive excerpts, coming releases, sales, free books, cover reveals and more.

Check out our complete list of authors, too!

No spam, no junk. That's a promise!

Sign Up Here

www.dragonbladepublishing.com

Dearest Reader;

Thank you for your support of a small press. At Dragonblade Publishing, we strive to bring you the highest quality Historical Romance from some of the best authors in the business. Without your support, there is no 'us', so we sincerely hope you adore these stories and find some new favorite authors along the way.

Happy Reading!

CEO, Dragonblade Publishing

Additional Dragonblade books by Author Jillian Eaton

Ladies of Seduction Series

The Duchess Takes a Lover (Book 1)

A duchess with nothing to lose . . .

After a disastrous wedding night followed by eighteen months of isolation at her husband's country estate, the Duchess of Southwick has grown tired of being lonely. There are only so many books a person can read, and Mara has read most of them twice. So she's made a decision. For the first time since her marriage, she's traveling to London for the Season. And while she's there, this meek, shy mouse of a wallflower who has never met a shade of beige she didn't like is going to do the unthinkable.

Mara Buxton, Duchess of Southwick, is going to take a lover.

A duke with everything to gain . . .

When Ambrose hears the rumors swirling about his wife, his initial reaction is scornful amusement. Mara, step out on him? Absurd. While a fiery spark of attraction first drew them together, it was extinguished long ago. The Duchess of Southwick, for all her beauty, is cold as ice, and the only thing she has a chance of inviting into her bed is snow. But when Ambrose discovers that she really does intend to have an affair, his amusement quickly turns to incredulity and then to jealousy. Mara is *his* wife, dammit.

If anyone is going to make her burn with passion . . . it's him.

PROLOGUE

March 1813
Lily & Grove Dress Shop, London, England

"H AVE YOU HEARD the news?" Lady Harmsworth asked in a hushed tone that was not very hushed at all. A loud, boisterous woman whose voice was outsized only by her bosom, she was incapable of whispering. Or of keeping any tidbit of gossip, no matter how small or inconsequential, to herself. As it so happened, there was nothing small *or* inconsequential about the rumor that she had been itching to divulge ever since she and the hard-of-hearing (for obvious reasons) Lord Harmsworth had arrived in London in advance of the much-anticipated Season.

"What news?" Lady Topple was quiet and as flat-chested as a piece of parchment, but she did like a good piece of tittle-tattle. Teetering on the verge of spinsterhood at the age of five and twenty with no prospects on the horizon (for obvious reasons), she lived vicariously through the scandalous lives of others . . . when she wasn't tending to her alarming number of felines.

"Is this in regard to that governess running away with the vicar? Because if it is, I've already heard it." Standing on a dais in the middle of the dress shop with her arms raised above her head as a seamstress circled around her with pins, Lady Farthing—the eldest of the trio—snapped her fingers and pointed at breasts that both time and six children had dragged down to an intolerable level. "Higher, dear. If they're not touching my chin then you're doing it wrong."

Lady Harmsworth gave a loud, vaguely insulted sniff. "*Everyone* has heard about the governess and the vicar. But what about the Duchess of Southwick?"

"The Duchess of Southwick?" Lady Topple repeated, looking confused. "What about her?"

"You've mixed up your names again," Lady Farthing said derisively. "The only thing interesting about the Duchess of Southwick is that she managed to land a duke. That girl is even more boring than Lady Topple, if such a thing is possible." She paused. "No offense meant, Lady Topple."

"None taken," Lady Topple mumbled, glancing at her lap and very much wishing she had thought to bring one of her cats.

"For your information, I *haven't* confused my names." Lady Harmsworth crossed her arms. "I have it on excellent authority that the Duchess of Southwick will be in town for the Season this year."

"That isn't *news*," said Lady Farthing. "That's what is expected of her. The bare minimum, really. And don't get me started on her wardrobe. Those bland colors she prefers never fail to make me nauseous. Why a woman married to the wealthiest man in England would willingly choose to subject herself to beige with *that* hair color is beyond me."

"She'll certainly never be renowned for her fashion," Lady Harmsworth agreed. "But maybe *this* will get her noticed." Her mouth curled in a conspiratorial smile. "The Duchess of Southwick is coming to London . . . and she plans to take a lover."

In the stunned silence that followed, someone could have heard a pin drop from the line of stitches that the seamstress was desperately making in an attempt to heave up Lady Farthing's bosom.

"That's absurd," Lady Farthing said at last, but there was just enough doubt in her tone to allow Lady Harmsworth's words to take root. For that was how gossip grew. In twisting vines and leaves, it slipped into whatever crack or crevice it was able to find. Then it stretched, and it expanded, until even the strongest, sharpest spade couldn't dig it out.

"She wouldn't dare," Lady Topple gasped. "She'll be ruined. The scandal—"

"Will be gargantuan." Lady Harmsworth licked her lips in anticipation. "I dare say even larger than when the Earl of Hollinbrook married his scullery maid after her belly began to swell. As if we were supposed to believe that she'd suddenly taken a liking to chocolate."

"*Higher*," Lady Farthing instructed the seamstress before she sighed with exasperation and yanked the needle and remaining pins out of the poor girl's hand. "Here, I'll do it myself." She ran a new piece of thread before turning her attention back to her friends. "Her husband would never allow such a thing. The Duke of Southwick, made a cuckold? When pigs take to the air, perhaps."

"He has a mistress," Lady Topple pointed out. "The French stage actress. I can't recall her name."

"By the time you do, he'll have already moved on to the next," Lady Farthing said with a touch of bitterness that did not go unnoticed by those in the room, all of whom were privy to the not-very-secret fact that Lord Farthing had a mistress of his own. "Because that is the privilege of men. To do as they please, with whom they please, whenever they please it. But a duchess should know better."

Lady Harmsworth shrugged. "Maybe she assumes that no one will find out. *I'm* not going to tell anyone. You know how I abhor gossip. Such a fickle business, spreading unsubstantiated claims of wrongdoing before they've even occurred. You can ruin someone's life that way."

"But . . ." Lady Topple picked at a scab on her neck where

one of her beloved cats had scratched her. "You just told us."

"Yes, but I'm not going to tell anyone *else.*" With a sniff, Lady Harmsworth turned up her nose. "Honestly, who do you take me for?"

BY NOON, THE news of the Duchess of Southwick's pending affair had traveled through seven notable households and a teahouse on Brunswick Street. The brewing scandal was on the tip of every tongue, and it was a horserace to share the titillating gossip with anyone that hadn't heard it yet.

By the dinner hour, there was hardly a person in Grosvenor Square and the surrounding boroughs that hadn't learned of the duchess's daring plan.

She was going to take a lover!

She was going to demand a divorce!

She was the king's secret mistress!

All right, no one *really* believed the last one. Mostly because King George was both blind and mad, and a little bit because it was well known that the Duchess of Southwick hadn't ventured away from her husband's country estate for the better part of eighteen months.

But the wild speculation was half the fun.

By half past midnight, the rumors had reached all the way to March House, a prestigious gentleman's club that specialized in high stakes gambling, beautiful women, and discretion. It swept through the elegant mahogany bars and across the felt card tables like wildfire, leaving a myriad of reactions in its wake.

Amazement.

Disbelief.

Shock.

One gentleman in particular, however, had a distinctly *different* response.

Tall and black haired, with blue eyes that could slice like a knife and a mouth capable of great cruelty, the Duke of Southwick merely lifted a brow when word of his wife's planned indiscretion traveled to the far corner of the club where he was lounging against a wall, drink in hand.

"You don't say," he murmured, and the Earl of Calvern, who had divulged the news, paled considerably when he realized to just whom he was speaking.

"I—I . . . please forgive me, Your Grace."

Southwick—better known to what close friends he had by his Christian name of Ambrose—sipped his brandy. "For what?"

A bead of sweat formed at the earl's receding hairline and began a slow, trickling descent. "Ah . . . I . . . that is . . ."

"You have not caused me undue offense, Calvern."

"I haven't?" Calvern expelled an audible sigh of relief. "Are you certain?"

Ambrose's smile did not touch the corners of his eyes. "If my darling wife manages to snare herself a lover, I'll be the first to offer my congratulations."

"I . . . I'm afraid I don't understand."

"The duchess is as cold as the ice that you're using to water down perfectly good brandy. There's no man in England who would want to climb into bed beside her." Ambrose drained what remained of his drink, then set the empty glass aside for a servant to pick up. "I know that I don't. If you'll excuse me, Calvern, I've spied a more entertaining companion over there."

The duke walked away, but his absence did nothing to diminish the rumors. If anything, his callous remarks—repeated in hushed tones again and again—enflamed them to a fever pitch, and by the end of the night all of London was on fire.

CHAPTER ONE

The Next Day
Southwick Castle, Derbyshire, England

C OMPLETELY OBLIVIOUS TO the gossip that was taking the *ton*
by storm, Marabelle Anne Buxton, Duchess of Southwick,
was in her rose garden with her hands in the cool spring soil
when her sister, Lady Katherine Colborne, came to call.

The siblings, three years apart in age, were as different as
night was from day. Demure and soft-spoken, Mara (as she
preferred to be called) enjoyed books, gardening, and composing
music while Kitty had always been drawn to more adventurous
activities including, but not limited to, horseback riding, tight-
rope walking, and sneaking out of her bedroom window to meet
any manner of midnight suitor.

Even their appearances were opposite, with Mara taking after
their father and Kitty their mother. As a result, Mara had dark
auburn hair, solemn brown eyes, and a willowy thin build while
Kitty was blonde, blue eyed, and voluptuous.

Then there was the little fact that Kitty was wildly in love
with her new husband, while Mara was . . . not.

"*There* you are," Kitty declared as she came skipping across
the lawn, the hem of her emerald-green traveling habit dragging

on what remained of the silvery morning frost. "I've been looking everywhere. I was half afraid that pack of wild dogs that's been roaming around ate you for their breakfast." She stopped, her nose wrinkling. "What are you doing?"

"If I don't remove the old growth, there won't be any room for new," Mara said calmly as she snipped off a dead rose and tossed it into the tin pail beside her. "So I'm pruning."

"Yes, I can see that." Gloved hands on her round hips, Kitty frowned down at her sister. "But why are *you* doing it? Where's your gardener? For heaven's sake, Mara. You're on your hands and knees. It's not seemly."

Swiping a bead of sweat from her brow, Mara sank onto her haunches, having been ready to take a rest even before Kitty arrived. The weather had been unseasonably warm and wet for early March. Generally this time of year she came out wearing a jacket, overcoat, and even a scarf. But today, with the sun uncovered by clouds, she wore only a light lace shawl over a plain brown dress that had witnessed many a spring gardening season.

"Who is here to see me besides you? Mr. Burrow is tending to the orchards over the hill, and both of his sons were needed elsewhere. We're reseeding the timothy fields today," she said with no small amount of pride. "For the most even rows, it's best if you have multiple people start off at the same—"

"I can assure you that I don't care," Kitty interrupted. "*Honestly*. Pruning roses. Seeding Thomas fields—"

"Timothy," Mara corrected automatically.

"—you're not a farmer, you're a duchess. You should be sipping tea in the parlor, not digging in the dirt in the garden!" A sprig of coiled yellow bounced across Kitty's cheek as she gave an agitated toss of her head. "Why did you bother to marry Southwick if you're just going to act as you always did? In case you haven't noticed, we needn't forage for our supper anymore."

A pang went through Mara.

A pang of loss. Of loneliness. Of lingering regret.

"You're right," she said, for often it was better to simply agree with her sister than try to argue. If Kitty said the sky was purple, you could either waste your breath trying to change her mind or you could smile, nod, and go about your day. "Would you like to go inside? We've a fresh delivery of figs. If you pair them with—"

"What I'd like," Kitty cut in, "is for you to explain why Lady Graham told *me* that Lady Bishop told *her* that the Baroness of Halifax overheard Lady Cartwright and Mrs. Shipley saying that you are planning to have an affair!"

"What?" Her head spinning—she must have been out in the sun longer than she'd thought—Mara placed her shears in the pail and rose slowly to her feet. She could have sworn she'd heard her sister say . . . but no. No, that wasn't possible. "They said *what*?"

Kitty grimaced. "Please don't make me repeat it."

"But . . ." She bit her bottom lip, a habit born of a childhood in which staying silent was the difference between a careless knock on the side of the head and a bruise that stayed black for days. "But I didn't tell anyone."

Her sister's jaw dropped open. "You mean it's *true*? Marabelle!"

"It's not true. But it's also not *untrue*. I . . . I need some water." She went inside with Kitty trailing behind her, firing off a litany of questions that she was incapable of answering. Finding a pitcher of freshly squeezed lemonade in the parlor, she excused the maid and poured a glass for herself, then one for her sister. "We should probably sit," she said, gesturing at a set of matching blue velvet armchairs. A partially open window admitted a light breeze that cooled her flushed cheeks as she contemplated the best way to explain herself . . . and her decision.

Adultery, the sheer betraying act of it, was not something that Mara would have *ever* considered under normal circumstances. But there was nothing normal about being rushed into a marriage to a man who intimidated her, enduring a wedding night that had terrified her, and being subsequently abandoned at a castle that had never felt like home.

For nearly two years she'd waited here.

She'd grown lonely here.

She'd *withered* here, like a rose left too long on the branch. Yearning, though yearning for what, precisely, she couldn't say. But she knew in her heart, in the depths of her being, that it wasn't this. That whatever she was meant to do with her life, it *wasn't this.* She had not survived the death of her mother and the abuse of her father to settle for isolation and desertion. For long days and even longer nights. Alone. Forgotten.

Forsaken.

"He never should have asked me to marry him," she said quietly, scratching at a spot of dirt on her skirt with her nail.

"What? Speak up," Kitty demanded. "You know I hate it when you mumble."

"Ambrose." Just speaking his name out loud made her tongue thicken and the tiny hairs on her nape tingle.

Ambrose Pierce Nathaniel Buxton, 6th Duke of Southwick.

A more domineering man she'd never met. When he had first approached her at the Glendale Ball, she'd assumed it was some sort of jest. Even a cruel prank. Then he'd asked her to dance, and who was she to refuse a duke? Swirling around in his arms, with every pair of eyes in the room pinned on her, she'd felt curiously weightless. As if her feet weren't quite touching the ground. Before she was able to fully catch her breath, the dance was over and he was gone. Until he materialized at her doorstep the next evening, an enormous bouquet of tulips in hand, to take her to the theater. They sat high in a box where more people watched them than the stage, and after the play was over, he kissed her.

Her, Lady Marabelle Holden, of average appearance and little to no social consequence.

It happened again the next day when he invited her on a carriage ride through Hyde Park. Kitty had come along as chaperone and had chattered away like a magpie the entire time while Mara had stared nervously at her lap, hardly daring to lift her chin and steal a peek at the man across from her for fear that if she did it would all turn out to be some elaborate illusion.

Except it wasn't, and it didn't, because he kissed her once more in Kensington Gardens, the memory of which still made her blush whenever she summoned it. Finally, he kissed her on their wedding day. Right on the mouth, for everyone in attendance to see. Hardly more than a brush, really, but oh, how her knees had quivered! In part from the shock of what was happening, but a little bit . . . a little bit because back then, she'd still fancied herself half in love with him.

Now she knew better.

"You're talking nonsense," Kitty scoffed. "Of course you should have married him. He's a *duke*, Mara."

Her hand trembled ever so slightly as she brought the lemonade to her lips and took a sip. "But he doesn't love me. I don't think he has *ever* loved me. Nor I . . . nor I him. Not in a real way. Not in a way that counted."

"Love?" Her sister's laugh was sharp and far too cynical for a woman of her age and beauty. "What does love have to do with marriage? Absolutely nothing," she replied before Mara could respond. "It's a fairytale spun up by those who didn't have to hide when they heard heavy footsteps on the stairs. Love is useless. Love is weakness. Love is what we should avoid, not strive for. Father loved Mama, and what did that get her? What did that get *us?*"

A rush of chills pressed ghostly fingertips down the length of Mara's spine. "Nothing," she whispered, but that wasn't completely true. Love, or at least their father's ill, twisted version of it, had got them plenty.

Bruises. Beatings. Brutality. Cowering behind doors and under beds with her hand pressed flush against Kitty's small mouth so that her sister wouldn't scream out and reveal their hiding place. Biting her tongue so hard that it bled and then crying herself to sleep with the taste of blood, wet and metallic, flooding her mouth. Silent tears, she reminded herself. Always silent, or else *he* would come.

The monster who had killed their mother in the name of

love.

That night when it happened—.

No. No, she wouldn't think of it. She *couldn't*.

That part of her life was over. She'd ended it when she accepted Ambrose's proposal . . . and unwittingly swapped one type of prison for another.

"He hasn't been here in months," she said, meeting Kitty's gaze over the rim of her glass. "I can barely recall the last time that we exchanged more than a handful of words. I'm sure he has a mistress in London. It's where he spends most of his time."

"I'm sure he does," Kitty shrugged. "They all do."

"Even William?" she asked, referring to her sister's husband of six months.

Kitty's face went blank, like a page being turned over. "I didn't come here to discuss William. I came here to find out why the entire *ton* is buzzing with news of your impending dalliance. You cannot *seriously* be considering taking a lover, Mara."

She looked away. "Would that be so inconceivable?"

"For me and most of the women of my acquaintance?" Her sister shook her head. "No. But for *you*? Yes. Don't you remember all of those times that you scolded me for climbing out the window? You've never met a rule that you didn't want to follow, and now you want to have an illicit affair? Whoever started this rumor has obviously never met you."

No, they probably hadn't. Aside from Kitty, she didn't have any close friends. And even then, sometimes Kitty felt more like an adversary than a confidant. She often grew weary of her sister's combative nature, but who else did she have to talk to, if not Kitty? No one else cared enough to come visit her.

Not even her own husband.

Inwardly bracing herself, she took another sip of lemonade. It was sweet on her tongue. So sweet that it made her want to throw up. Or maybe that was just her own nerves.

"But what if . . . what if it's true?" she said.

"What's true?" Kitty asked, wandering over to a shelf and

picking up a crystal sculpture of a lotus flower; it was but one of a hundred wedding presents that had been dropped off at the castle after Ambrose made it clear he didn't want them littering his residence in London.

"The rumor."

Tossing the crystal flower from one hand to the other, Kitty laughed. "Don't be absurd. You wouldn't." Then she glanced over her shoulder at Mara's face and her eyes widened. "Tell me you wouldn't. If Southwick found out—"

"I didn't tell anyone. There's no one here *to* tell." She rose from her seat and poured herself more lemonade, more out of anxious habit than any desire to drink. When she offered to do the same for Kitty, her sister shook her head again and frowned.

"You must have told someone, because it's all that anyone is talking about. It's only a matter of time before your husband finds out. Mara, this is *not* how affairs are done. You're supposed to make *some* attempt at discretion."

"I had planned to make *all* the attempts! I didn't want people to know, least of all Ambrose." The mere idea of her husband being cognizant of what she was planning filled her with dread. She could already picture his reaction. Those icy blue eyes raking across her with thinly veiled contempt. The disapproving pulse of his jaw. "*Another disappointment, Marabelle. Why am I not surprised?*"

"I'm just so lonely, Kitty," she said despairingly. "Trapped here in this large, empty house all on my own. I want companionship. I want to discuss my day. I want to fall asleep next to someone at night." She squeezed her eyes shut as the truth was squeezed from her. "I want someone to know that I exist."

"*I* know that you exist, and this house isn't empty, Mara. It's filled to the brim with furniture, clothes, paintings, jewels! Why, look at that diamond pendant around your neck. It's enormous," said Kitty, not bothering to hide her envy. "You have everything we ever dared dream of, and you want to risk it all for what? Some nameless lover who will keep you entertained for the span of a few weeks before Southwick has every bone in his body broken and you banished to some cottage in Scotland, never to be seen or heard from again? Don't be absurd."

"It's not absurdity to want attention, and Ambrose isn't going to care. He hasn't cared about anything else I've done for more than a year and a half, or even bothered to inquire into my well-being since Christmas. I could be dying or dead, for all he knows." When bitterness threatened to creep into her tone, she swallowed it down. This was exactly why she wanted to seek out a male companion. So that she *didn't* become hard, resentful, and discontented. So she didn't become . . . well, so she didn't become like her husband. "You said it yourself. Women in our situations have affairs all the time. It's practically expected."

"Yes, but you're not like the rest of us."

As Mara had always been plagued by the notion that she didn't quite fit in with her peers no matter how hard she tried, that little sentence stung more than it should have.

"How is that?" she asked, shifting her weight from one leg to the other.

"You're mannerly and decorous. Exasperatingly so." Kitty flung out an arm. "And having relations with a man who is not your husband is bad. Entertaining, certainly. Wickedly exciting. But very bad."

"I wouldn't have relations with him," she exclaimed, startled. "Why would you say that?"

Her sister eyed her closely. "Mara, what do you think an affair entails, precisely?"

"Spending time together?" she ventured.

"Time in *bed*, you mean. Naked."

"Nak . . . no. No, no." Blushing from the roots of her hair to the middle of her décolletage, Mara stumbled back to her chair and slid bonelessly into it. "I wouldn't . . . that is . . . I don't want that. I hate that."

Kitty's lips twisted in a humorless smile. "You hate fucking and it's the only thing that William and I are any good at. Maybe we should just switch husbands. I'm *jesting*," she said when Mara's mouth dropped open. "Trust me, you wouldn't want him. Although there's no denying that Ambrose has a certain dark appeal. You know, I must admit that I was caught off guard when you announced your engagement. He never struck me as the sort of man that you'd ever be interested in."

"He wasn't." On a sigh, Mara let her head slump back. "Until he told me I was pretty."

And I was foolish enough to believe him.

CHAPTER TWO

April 1811
Glendale Manor, London, England

"**M**ARA, PUT DOWN your book," Kitty hissed in her ear. "The Duke of Southwick is coming this way!"

Blinking, Mara used a silk hair ribbon to save her spot before deftly sliding the book under her seat. A ballroom wasn't exactly an ideal place to read, but what else was she supposed to do for five long hours while her sister's dance card filled and hers remained conspicuously empty? Well, empty that is except for Lord Stapleton, but as he smelled vaguely of mincemeat jam and had a habit of trouncing on her instep whenever they attempted to execute a right-hand turn, she didn't count him.

"Who is coming this way?" she asked, craning her neck around her sister's skirt. The pink gown had been boxy and downright frumpy when she'd worn it for her debut last year, with clumps of lace in all the wrong places and bell sleeves the size of overgrown eggplants. But Kitty, skilled with a needle and blessed with an eye for design, had changed the dress into an elegant, flowing work of art that barely resembled the garment that had earned Mara more than a few snickers.

Kitty had offered to work her magic on Mara's gown for

tonight's festivities, a daisy-yellow dress that had once belonged to their Aunt Sarah (notable for both her hideous taste in fashion and love of crumpets), but Mara had politely declined. Yes, the dress was clearly too big and yes, the color was blinding. But the cotton fabric was cool and the waistline was comfortable, and what did it matter what she looked like as no one was going to bother looking at her?

When her sister was around, Mara wasn't merely in her shadow. She was the dust under the rug beneath the sofa in her shadow. And she didn't mind. Not really. For she *wanted* Kitty to find a match. She wanted her sister to escape, to leave their hellish house and never have to come back. But the only way to do that was to marry. The only way to marry was to find a husband. The only way to find a husband was to attend a ball.

And yes, she needed a husband, too.

She needed to escape, too.

But she'd made a promise to their mother that she would protect Kitty . . . and it was a promise she meant to keep. Even if it came at the expense of her own life.

Another reason she favored the ugly yellow dress?

It covered her bruises.

"The Duke of Southwick." Bouncing excitedly on her heels, Kitty abruptly whipped around. "How is my face? Do I look all right?" She peeled back her lips. "Anything in my teeth?"

"You look beautiful," Mara responded truthfully.

In the soft light of the chandeliers swinging above their heads, her sister's countenance was glowing. Her blue eyes sparkled, her blonde hair shone, and even her teeth were squeaky clean. By comparison, Mara felt pale and withdrawn, like a rose that had been denied the sunlight.

Her hair hung lank around her shoulders, her mouth was unconsciously pinched shut for fear of revealing her crooked incisor, and there were dark smudges under her eyes from spending the night awake and watching their bedroom door.

"A *duke*, Mara." Kitty sucked in a breath. "This could change *everything.* Oh, he's getting closer! Don't *stare* at him. Goodness!"

But it was too late. She was already staring.

How could she not?

The Duke of Southwick was, in a single word, menacing. And if she had two? *Terrifyingly handsome.*

He was tall, with broad shoulders and a flat abdomen and muscular thighs encased in black trousers. As a matter of fact, his entire ensemble was black, from his coat to his boots to his cravat. Even his *hair* was black and swept cleanly off his temple, giving her a clear, unhindered view of his face.

Slashing brows, a straight nose, firm lips, a strong jaw.

And his eyes . . .

Mara swallowed nervously.

His eyes were pale blue glass, sharp and ruthlessly assessing as they performed a cursory examination of her sister before settling squarely on her.

As Kitty's older sister and chaperone, the duty fell to Mara to initiate the introductions. But when she rose—unsteadily—from her chair, she found that her tongue had stuck to the roof of her mouth and the best she could manage was an unintelligible, "*Uggrrr.*" Then Kitty kicked her quite hard, and the flash of pain pried her tongue loose enough for her to sputter, "Your—Your Grace, might I introduce my sister, Lady Katherine H-Holden."

The duke's impenetrable gaze flicked to Kitty, then promptly returned to Mara.

"What is your name?" he asked in a deep, rich voice that could have made the devil blush.

"M-Mara. Marabelle. Lady Marabelle Holden."

Kitty stepped in front of her and dropped into an elaborate curtsy that gave the duke a clear view of her ample bosom. "What an unexpected pleasure it is to make your acquaintance, Your Grace," she purred whilst fluttering her lashes.

"Indeed." He shifted his weight. "Lady Marabelle, have you room on your dance card?"

Mara froze. "My—*my* dance card?"

The Duke of Southwick gave a curt, impatient nod. It was obvious that he was not a man accustomed to having to repeat himself and the act of doing so was an irritant. It was also obvious that he must have recently suffered a blow to the head. Why on earth else would he be ignoring Kitty and speaking directly to Mara? No one ever spoke directly to Mara. They talked past her. Over her. Around her. Through her as if she weren't even in the room.

But *to* her?

Never.

If Kitty's bewildered expression was any indication, she was equally puzzled.

"I . . . I have room." Mara bit the inside of her cheek. "Lots of room."

"But I've only two dances left," said Kitty with a coquettish toss of her head. "If you'd like to claim one, Your Grace, I'd dare to suggest that you act quickly lest I be forced to disappoint you."

Relief washed over Mara. That was how it was meant to happen. Strikingly imposing gentlemen danced with her sister, and she was left alone to read the books that she'd snuck in under her voluminous skirts. But then why . . . why was the Duke of Southwick reaching his hand out toward *her*?

His jacket sleeve pulled back, exposing an inch of bronzed skin between his black glove and his cuff. "Can I have it? Your card. I should like to sign my name."

Mara jerked her gaze away from his wrist and a slid a frantic glance at Kitty who stood frozen in place, her eyes—a shade lighter than her sister's with flecks of green—bulging in an unflattering manner.

"Umm . . . I . . . ." She patted her sides, then turned to look at her chair. "I'm not sure where it is. Maybe . . . maybe you should sign your name to my sister's instead?" she suggested hopefully.

"Or we can skip such formalities and you can accompany me onto the floor before the next contra-dance begins."

"Right—right now?" she squeaked.

He raised a brow. "Have you somewhere pressing to be?"

"No. No, I, umm, it's just—"

"Go on," said Kitty with an airy laugh and a not-very-gentle shove that nearly sent her stumbling. "His Grace is asking you to dance, Mara. You wouldn't want to insult him by declining, would you?"

Mara wet her dry lips. With enormous trepidation and a knot in her stomach the size of the Atlantic, she slowly placed her fingertips on the edge of the duke's outstretched arm. An immediate tingle, the kind she received whenever she dashed across a rug in her stockinged feet, shot through her. On a gasp, she lifted her chin to find the duke staring down at her, a notched line in the middle of his temple.

"Lady Marabelle?" he asked, his tone noticeably rougher than it had been a moment ago. "Are you all right?"

"I'm . . . I'm fine," she said faintly, which of course she wasn't, but what other answer was there to give? Kitty was right. She couldn't snub someone as powerful and influential as the Duke of Southwick by refusing his offer to dance. No matter that he must have mistaken her for someone else. Someone of consequence. Someone of interest. Someone of beauty.

He began to walk and she followed, her natural gate hindered by the sheer size of her gown. She tripped twice before he pivoted to face her, a hint of ire in his gaze. All around them couples squared off into position to prepare for the ever-so popular contra-dance, and when the band started to play the introduction, signaling the dance was about to begin, Mara and the duke did the same.

"If this is an act," he said, his mouth hovering beside her ear as his hand settled on her waist, "I commend you on your originality."

"An act?" she said, confused both by his statement and where *her* hand was supposed to go. On his side, she knew that much from her lessons, but where?

Too low, and she would be encroaching on his hip. Too high,

and her thumb would be intimately close to his chest. She'd never seemed to have this quandary with Lord Hamsworth, but to compare the two men would be to stand a pudgy walrus and an elegant panther side by side. One was round and fancied fish. The other hard and dangerously fierce.

"A display meant to gain attention. Surely you cannot be *this* clumsy." He gave her a wry look before solving her dilemma by grabbing hold of her wrist and placing it in the middle of his ribcage. For an instant longer than it should have, the pad of his thumb rested over her racing pulse and her heart gave a rapid *thump* as another tingle ricocheted through her.

"I am not trying to be clumsy," she said, frowning up at him. "It's this dress."

"Are you referring to the potato sack that you're wearing?"

"My aunt gave it to me."

"Does she dislike you?"

Before Mara was able to muster a reply, everyone was required to switch partners, and she found herself facing an earl whose pragmatic touch failed to elicit even so much as a prickle. Then she was back with the Duke of Southwick, so darkly attractive, and this time she noticed that she wasn't the only one unwillingly captivated by his ruthless charm.

"Why is everyone staring?" she asked, rising onto her toes in order to peer over his shoulder as he spun her in an arcing circle before bringing her in close, his grip on her waist tightening.

"They're wondering who you are and why I am dancing with you."

"Why *are* you dancing with me?"

"Because I haven't before."

"You haven't danced with my sister, either," she felt compelled to point out.

His sigh stirred the tendrils behind her ear as they passed close. "Yes, I have. A hundred times over."

They executed a spin, broke apart, and returned to each other.

"No," she said, a tad breathlessly. "I'm nearly sure that you haven't. Because if you had, it's all that she would talk about."

The corners of his mouth curled into a shape caught halfway between a smile and a smirk. "Are *you* going to talk about our dance, Lady Marabelle?"

"That depends," she said truthfully.

"On what?"

"On whether this is a dream or really happening."

He chuckled. The sound of his laughter was rusty and somewhat hoarse, as if he didn't do it very often. And maybe he didn't. The duke did not strike her as a man particularly given to idle amusements.

"This is no dream, I can assure you of that."

"How can you be certain?"

"Because," he murmured, bowing his head until his mouth skimmed across her cheek, "if it were, you wouldn't be wearing this awful gown. You wouldn't be wearing anything at all."

Stunned, Mara stopped in her tracks just as the dance concluded. The ballroom erupted into applause, but in the midst of the noise and the mayhem of lords and ladies searching for their next partner, her wide-eyed gaze remained locked on the duke as a rush of heat pooled low in her belly.

"I plan to call on you tomorrow at your residence," he said, and it wasn't a question or a request, but a statement. A *demand*. "Wear something other than this, if you please. You're far too pretty to hide behind a mountain of fabric."

Then he was gone, and Mara—poor, ignorant, innocent Mara—was smitten.

CHAPTER THREE

March 1813
75 Mill Lane, London, England

AMBROSE DID NOT hate his wife.

There were some, he knew, who assumed he did, assumed that was why he and Mara had rarely been seen in the same place together since their nuptials. But what they did not understand was that hate was an emotion that required great feeling, not dissimilar to love. And Ambrose was a man incapable of feeling either.

Not to say he hadn't in the past.

When he was a lad, around eight years of age, he had developed a great fondness for a dog that he'd found roaming through the woods of Southwick Castle. The dog—which he'd named Wags—had been so thin that Ambrose was able to count all his ribs. Having never been allowed to keep a pet before, he'd fallen instantly in love with the scruffy hound. But as he was aware of what his father would say if he asked for permission to keep Wags, he'd hidden the dog away in an empty stall in the stable and for weeks kept his secret pet fed with scraps of food from the kitchen.

Under the cloak of darkness, Ambrose and Wags had romped

together through the fields and explored the abandoned remnants of a nearby cottage that the local villagers swore was haunted. Ambrose would bring books out to the stable and read aloud to Wags for hours. On occasion, he'd even lost track of the time and fallen asleep curled up beside his pet.

Over the duration of the summer, Wags became his confidant, his companion, and the only friend of a little boy who had none. Until one day, when Ambrose went to the stall and found his father standing beside the open door and the groundskeeper standing beside him, a hunting rifle resting on his left shoulder.

"Where . . . where is Wags?" he asked, even though in the pit of his stomach he already knew.

"That flea-ridden mongrel has been disposed of," his father said coolly. "Would you care to explain yourself, Ambrose?"

"Wags wasn't hurting anyone!" At his sides, Ambrose's small hands knotted into impotent fists of rage. How he yearned to use them against his father! But the duke loomed large, as big as a mountain, and his power was without limit. Ambrose could no more strike him than he could the sun. "You didn't have to kill him. I would have found him a different home!"

"You never should have found him at all." Most men would have been moved by the glistening of tears in their young child's eyes. But the duke had seemed to feel nothing more than a mild twinge of disgust. "The dog's blood is on your hands, Ambrose. Let this be a warning. Follow the rules I've set forth or suffer the consequences. Now go inside and get ready for dinner. The Wentworths will be joining us and you'll be on your best behavior . . . or else."

With his eyes wet and his chest aching, Ambrose had bolted out of the stables.

My fault, he thought as he ran.

My fault, my fault, my fault.

If not for him, Wags would still be alive. The dog had trusted him, and he'd betrayed that trust by getting him killed. It was a brutal, hard-earned lesson. To love something was to endure the pain of losing it. And on that day, at the tender age of eight, Ambrose decided that he never wanted to feel that pain again.

It was a lesson he'd carried with him into adulthood. As he had stood over his father's grave with rain lashing at his back and his weeping mother holding onto his arm, he hadn't been overwhelmed with the fury he'd once experienced as a helpless boy.

He hadn't been joyful or sad.

He hadn't been melancholy.

He hadn't been regretful.

He had been . . . nothing. Well, nothing but vaguely annoyed that his mother was wiping her face on his new coat.

Six months after assuming his sire's title, Ambrose sent the dowager duchess to live at a cottage estate several hours from Southwick Castle. He paid for her every expense including a staff of twenty, dutifully wrote her a letter four times a year, and otherwise forgot that she existed. Much as she had done for the entirety of his adolescence.

On the one-year anniversary of the duke's demise, he'd set about finding himself a wife. The requirements were clear. He needed a woman of excellent breeding who was passable in appearance and meek in nature. A woman who would bear him an heir and then leave him alone. After a brief search, he found Lady Marabelle Holden.

The red-haired, doe-eyed eldest daughter of a viscount was plainer than he would have liked, but she was quiet and shy, and she didn't babble incessantly about fashion or the weather. He courted her for less than a month. They were married in May, and by June they were already estranged . . . just as he'd wanted.

The only thing that hadn't gone according to his meticulously crafted plan was that Mara's belly remained devoid of child. But in order to put a babe there he'd have to repeat their wedding night, and since *that* wasn't going to happen, he'd pushed off the matter of his heir to some undetermined time in the future.

With another Season rapidly approaching, Ambrose had been

giving serious consideration to traveling abroad. Sans wife, of course. Maybe a mistress, although he'd not kept one of those since taking a duchess. Not out of any sense of loyalty or obligation to his vows; rather he hadn't desired the headache. A mistress was all well and good *in* bed, but out of it previous experience had revealed that the endless requests for jewels, finery, and (worst of all) attention weren't equal to the pleasure gained from such an arrangement.

He had a hand, didn't he? And while it wasn't comparable to the clench of a tight, wet quim, it was better than the fake tears of a female as she begged him not to leave.

And the *clinging*.

Behind his desk, Ambrose gave a shudder. How he abhorred the clinging.

Taking a drink of coffee, he began to sort through the correspondence piled high in the center of his desk. The morning ritual set him up for a day of organized tasks that began with the post and culminated in a brandy at March House, for if there was anything that Ambrose *did* enjoy, it was routine.

Flipping through the various letters, invitations, and invoices, he paused when he came across an ivory envelope decorated in Mara's unmistakably elegant handwriting. He was unable to recall the last letter he'd received from his wife. Come to think of it, he was unable to recall the last time they'd occupied the same room.

Christmas, perhaps?

No, he'd spent Christmas here, at Mill House, a four-tier residence that bordered the northwest corner of Hyde Park.

November, then, or maybe October.

A year.

Devil take it, had it really been that long?

Reaching for his paper knife, a sleek piece of silver inscribed with his initials, Ambrose sliced open the wax seal and removed the folded piece of paper within. *It smells like her*, was his initial thought. Lilacs in bloom.

Mara had always smelled like lilacs in bloom, even on the night they met.

Then he read the actual letter, and his second thought was *the fuck she is.*

It started benignly enough. Pleasant, even.

My Lord Duke,

I do hope that this letter finds you in good spirits and even better health. The estate is doing well, and spring crops have been planted with high yields expected. Come summer and autumn, we should have a wonderful harvest season.

In a different vein, I feel compelled to be forthright with you in a matter that I never planned to become public knowledge. As you may or may not have heard, I will be traveling to London for the upcoming Season. You needn't worry that I'll encroach upon your privacy; I have already made arrangements to stay with my sister and her husband, Lord Wycroft, at their townhouse in Mayfair. But I must confess, that is not my sole reason for putting ink to parchment.

After much consideration, I have decided to take a lover.

As someone who has undoubtedly enjoyed the company of paramours, both before our marriage and during it, I hope this does not offend or cause you a great deal of shock. On the contrary, I should like to believe this will be a relief in that you needn't concern yourself with enduring my company, something that you have made clear is disagreeable to your constitution.

Naturally, I shall employ every act of discretion at my disposal. It is not my wish to cause you embarrassment or harm.

I should like to thank you in advance for your understanding.

Respectfully,
Marabelle Southwick

"HUMPHREY!" Ambrose roared, slowly crumpling the letter into a ball.

Accustomed to being summoned via bell, his butler of half a

decade almost tripped over a scullery maid in his haste to reach the study.

"Your—Your Grace?" he said, presenting himself in the open doorway. "How can I be of service?"

"Have my valet pack me a traveling bag, Humphrey, and have the landau brought round."

The butler's quick blink was his only sign of surprise. "I take it you've chosen between Portugal and Albania?"

"Neither," he said shortly. "I'm traveling to Southwick Castle."

"Southwick Castle, Your Grace?" This time, Humphrey didn't even attempt to disguise his astonishment. It was well known, at least among the staff, that the duke detested his ancestral family home. During Humphrey's five-year tenure, he was able to count on one hand the number of times Ambrose had visited the 500-acre country estate. "But . . . why?"

"Because," Ambrose began, his voice quiet and all the more dangerous for it, "the duchess and I need to have a conversation. See to it that my belongings are prepared and the carriage is readied with all haste."

"Right away, Your Grace."

"Excellent." He opened a gold inkwell and reached across his desk for a blank piece of parchment. "Oh, and Humphrey?"

The butler straightened. "Yes, Your Grace?"

"Don't ask me a personal question ever again, or it will be the last time you do so under my employment."

"Yes, Your Grace."

🙥🙥🙥🙣🙣🙣

BLISSFULLY OBLIVIOUS TO the storm that was on its way to her, Mara was on *her* way to the house of a local farmer whose wife had recently given birth.

Kitty, staying through the end of the week, had chosen to

remain behind in the parlor with the gossip papers while Mara filled a basket with honey, bread, and cheese before heading out.

Mara walked briskly, enjoying the feel of the sun on her face and the breeze in her hair. Untethered by ribbon or pin, her curls swung down her back in a runaway waterfall of sun-streaked copper beneath a straw bonnet. She had a lady's maid to help her dress and fashion a tidy coiffure, but with no visitors and no husband to admonish her untidy appearance, she preferred stealing the time traditionally used on readying herself for the day and spending it on something else. Like bringing food to a family with another mouth to feed.

The door to the sagging cottage sprang open before Mara could knock, and three children popped out, their eyes widening with delight at the sight of the treats that she'd brought.

"Hello," she said politely, resting the basket on her hip. "Is your mother or father at home?"

"Papa went into town," said the tallest child, a lanky boy with a shock of white-blond hair sticking out of a plain brown cap. "But Mama is here. She's in bed with the baby."

"We have a sister!" chimed the middle child, a girl with round cheeks and braids.

"New sissy," said the third, another boy who couldn't have been older than two. Sticking his thumb in his mouth, he began to suck noisily.

"How wonderful! Congratulations." Smiling, Mara knelt to their level and held out the basket. "Would you mind taking this to her? There's bread and cheese, and I think if you dig around a little bit, you may even find a peppermint or three."

Giving a loud whoop of excitement, the oldest boy grabbed the basket and loped off with the smallest toddling behind. But the girl remained, her head tilting to the side as she studied Mara with a child's somber intensity.

"Yes?" Mara asked, sensing the girl had a question. "What is it?"

If her wedding night hadn't been such a complete and utter

disaster, she liked to think that *she* might have a little girl by now. A little girl to nurture and teach. A little girl to love. A little girl to raise the way she wished she and Kitty had been raised. With patience, understanding, and a parent's unwavering devotion.

Tentatively, the girl reached out and patted one of Mara's loose curls. "Are you a princess?" she whispered.

"A princess?" Mara repeated with a startled laugh. "What makes you say that?"

"You *look* like a princess."

"I'm sorry to disappoint you. I'm not a princess. But you could be."

The girl gasped. "Really?"

"Oh, yes. But there are three rules you must follow."

She nodded solemnly. "I'm good at following rules. Mama says so. But my brothers aren't. They don't *ever* listen."

Mara bit back a grin. "First, a princess is always kind and helps those in need. Can you be kind and helpful, especially for your mother and new sissy?"

Still holding onto a strand of Mara's hair, the girl bounced excitedly up and down. "Yes, yes, I can!"

"Excellent. Secondly, a princess must love animals."

"*I* love animals!"

"Very good. And thirdly, and this is the most important . . . a princess must always believe in herself, no matter what." Gently extricating her hair from the girl's grasp, Mara tapped her on the nose and then stood. "If you can do those three things, then you, my lady, are a princess. Now why don't you go inside before your mother begins to wonder where you are and your brothers eat your peppermint."

Beaming from ear to ear, the girl scampered away into the house and Mara set out for Southwick Castle. It would have been far quicker to take a carriage, but she didn't mind walking. At least not until it started to rain.

The weather between the end of winter and the beginning of spring was unpredictable at best and tumultuous at worst, the sky blue one minute and black the next, the air calm and then wild as a tempest. When she'd left the castle, it had been warm. Hot, even. That was why she'd left her pelisse at home, exposing her arms to the sunlight. Somewhere along the way she'd even lost her bonnet, leaving her wearing nothing more than her undergarments and a faded beige dress with short sleeves and a shortened hem for easier range of movement.

A spattering of raindrops came first. Big, fat plops of water that had her increasing her step to a half walk, half run. But before she'd gone more than a handful of yards, the heavens parted and a deluge sprang forth.

With a shriek, Mara took off toward the closest natural shelter she could spy through the sheets of rain: a towering oak tree with limbs so large they stretched across the entire lane. Pressing her back flat against the trunk, she hugged herself for warmth while berating her foolishness for not being better prepared. She'd lived in this rolling stretch of countryside for more than a year and a half and knew how fast the weather was capable of changing. She should have worn a Spencer jacket, or at very least a shawl. And where was her hat? In a puddle now, most likely, and her throat clogged with fear as she imagined how she would explain away the waste.

"What do you mean, you've lost a glove?" Eriam Holden's face contorted in rage as he advanced on his daughter, the flat of his palm already raised.

"I'm . . . I'm sorry, Papa." Tearfully apologetic, Mara willed her feet to remain rooted to the creaking floorboards. It was worse when she ran. It was always worse when she ran. "I'm not sure what happened to it. I'll—I'll go search again, in the morn—"

"You ungrateful little brat. Do you've any idea how much those gloves cost?" Eriam's hand flew through the air.

Shuddering, Mara pulled herself from the memory—but one of a hundred exactly like it—and forced herself to return to the present where money was no object and her father no longer loomed in the shadows, the stench of gin staining his breath, waiting for an excuse to release his vile hatred for himself onto his two defenseless children.

Eriam Holden had drawn his last earthly breath seven months ago, but it didn't matter. When a monster died, it didn't disappear. Instead, it was relegated to moments of fear and the dregs of nightmares where it laid in wait, claws extended and teeth sharp.

As she waited for the rain to subside, Mara purposefully changed her focus to other things. Like the cup of hot tea that was awaiting her at home, and the book she'd recently started, and—

The churn of carriage wheels on gravel made her heart jump. She hadn't expected anyone else to be out in such unforgiving elements, but since they were, maybe they could give her a ride to the castle! Slicking her hair behind her ears, she sprang out from under the tree and ran to the road, her wet skirts slapping at her legs as she waved her arms in the air.

"Wait!" she yelled at the black landau slowly making its way along the lane, its occupants obscured behind a high window covered in a swath of red fabric. "Wait, please!"

Having spotted her, the driver—perched atop a riser seat in front of the carriage and looking just as miserable as Mara felt— hauled on the reins and the matching team of gray draft horses came to a plodding halt.

"Miss, do you require assistance?" he called out, cupping his hands around his mouth so that his voice carried over the relentless downpour.

"Yes!" With relief coursing through her and rain coursing down her back, Mara slid down a small embankment and stumbled into the road. She was shivering and soaked to the skin but elated that rescue had come. At least before the door swung open . . . and her husband glared out.

CHAPTER FOUR

"AMBROSE." MARA'S ARMS fell limply to her sides. "What—what are you doing here?"

"What am *I* doing here?" he said, his contemptuous gaze traveling from her knotted hair to her mud-streaked skirts. "What in God's name are *you* doing here? It's pouring."

"Thank you," she said icily. "I hadn't noticed."

A muscle ticked in his jaw. "Get in the carriage, Mara."

She shook her head even as her teeth began to chatter. "I'd r-rather not."

"Don't be a fool." He opened the door wider and gave a short, impatient jerk of his arm. "You'll freeze to death out there."

Would you even care, she wanted to ask, but dared not.

"I prefer to w-walk," she said instead. "I'll meet you at the c-c-castle."

She had never defied him before.

Not openly.

But if his absence had given her anything, it was clarity. A wife's obedience only went so far and then it had to be earned. She had to *want* to listen to Ambrose, to trust that he had her best interests at heart, and she didn't.

Because her husband didn't *have* a heart.

Or if he did, it was buried so deep down inside that it had turned to stone a long time ago.

Blinking water from her lashes, she started to walk away from the landau. Yes, it was cold, wet, and the rain showed no signs of ceasing. But she'd prefer to drown in a puddle than sit beside Ambrose in a carriage.

Without warning, a hand clamped onto her elbow and spun her around. She caught a glimpse of furious blue eyes and then Ambrose was dragging her back to the horses despite her best efforts to resist.

"Let me go!" she cried, clawing at the fingers wrapped around her arm like iron manacles.

"When I told you to get in the carriage," Ambrose said through clenched teeth, "it was not a request."

No, it never was.

The Duke of Southwick didn't *ask* for anything.

He took it.

The driver looked the other way as he shoved her up the steps and onto a padded bench seat. She landed awkwardly, her fall cushioned by the landau's sumptuous upholstery, and had barely managed to right herself before he slammed the door shut and threw himself into the opposite seat.

"You're terrible," she said, glaring at him through a veil of tangled curls.

"You're welcome," he retorted as the carriage began to move at a snail's pace to account for the torrents of rain on the roof and road.

Mara swallowed a groan of despair.

At this rate, they'd be trapped together in close proximity for an hour or more!

"I was perfectly capable of walking." The inside of the landau was dry, but her clothes were soaked through and becoming colder by the second. Instinctively seeking to warm herself, she hugged her knees to her chest, and didn't that make for a sorry sight? The Duchess of Southwick, wet and bedraggled, while her indescribably awful husband lorded over her.

She hated that he was handsome.

Hated that he exuded power with every breath.

Hated that he could snap his fingers and people would do whatever he wanted.

But she especially hated that even now, even after their wretched wedding night and his subsequent abandonment, there was a piece of her that still quivered whenever she was near him. It always had, and she feared that it always would. For no matter how much she hated him, that traitorous piece of her loved him desperately. Like a splinter jammed under her nail that she couldn't pry loose.

"You're shivering," he noted with a scowl, as if her discomfort was somehow a plague on *him*. "Take my greatcoat."

"No, I don't want—fine," she muttered below her breath when he ignored her refusal and, leaning forward, draped the heavy garment over her shoulders, enclosing her in his achingly familiar scent, a combination of cedarwood from his cologne water and a tangy hint of citrus from his shaving lather.

"Were you walking from your lover or to him?" he asked after he'd sat back, and beneath the oversized coat Mara flushed a deep, blotchy red from her temple all the way to her toes.

"You received my letter." And why, why, *why* did the post have to be quick *this* time? She'd sent the letter with the hope that it would arrive in London right before she did in an effort to avoid this very scenario. But of course that would require luck, and while she had the bad variety in spades, she'd yet to find a pinch of good.

Ambrose slowly tapped his fingers on his thigh, not unlike a cat twitching its tail right before it pounced on an unsuspecting mouse. "I did. Tell me, dear wife, are you suffering from a disease or other sort of malady?"

"Disease?" she said, confused. "Why would you—"

"Have you fallen recently and struck your head?"

"No, I—"

"Then the only other explanation is lunacy."

"Lunacy?" She clutched her damp skirts. "I'm not . . . I'm not *insane.*"

He smiled that vague, empty, cold smile that never failed to send a shiver along her spine. "But you must be, to think that I'd willingly turn a blind eye to your infidelity."

Having prepared herself for this conversation—albeit not this soon or in these circumstances—she was ready with a reply. "What do you care what I do, Ambrose? I said that I would be discreet, and I meant it! You needn't have come all the way here. You haven't before, and that's the problem, isn't it?" His coat slipped over her shoulders as she pitched to the edge of her seat. "You married me and then sent me away while you continued to enjoy all of your old pursuits. Carousing with women, drinking, gambling—"

"I've not slept with anyone since we said our vows," he interrupted. "The rest, well . . ." His shoulders lifted in a carelessly brusque shrug. "Guilty as charged."

"Am I truly meant to believe that?" she scoffed even as her heart gave a pitifully joyous flutter.

"Believe whatever you'd like. It matters naught." His eyes narrowed. "What *does* matter is your public pursuit of an affair. You've set tongues wagging from Derbyshire to Dublin. If you really planned to take a lover, Mara, you should have been more careful who you told."

Indignation sparked in her breast. "I didn't *tell* anyone, and I *do* plan to—to go through with it!"

"You can stop the act," he drawled, his tone infuriatingly dismissive. As if she were a child or a servant, and wasn't that how he'd always treated her? Certainly never as his equal, and never as a wife. Not really. Not in any of the ways that mattered. "You got what you wanted. I'm here, and I'll be remaining here until such time as we depart for London. We'll go together to stave off the rumors, make a few appearances, and then you'll unfortunately take ill and have to return to Southwick Castle for the remainder of the Season."

Mara stared at him, disbelief shuttering her expression. "Is that . . . is that why you think I'm doing this? That this is all some elaborate scheme in an attempt to draw you out here?"

His mouth twisted in a smirk. "Why else?"

For company, she wanted to shout. *For a man to look at me like I am someone special instead of a burden they have to endure. For laughter. For friendship. For the butterflies I used to get in my belly when you at least pretended that you cared.*

"We're here," she said instead, and was out the door and hurrying up the front steps before the carriage had even come to a full stop.

AMBROSE'S BROW FURROWED as he watched his wife flee into the massive tomb of a mansion that he had deliberately avoided since inheriting it. Halfway there, she dropped his coat in a puddle, causing a rare grin to flit across his face.

Mara was far bolder than he remembered. Brazen, even.

She was also beautiful.

No, not beautiful, he thought as he departed the carriage. *Fucking gorgeous.*

Mara had never been ugly, but her shyness—hunched shoulders, aversion to eye contact, clothes that were obviously too big—had given the illusion of a dull, quiet little kitten. A little kitten, that, over the course of his absence, had evolved into a fiery tigress complete with a wild red mane and a dress plastered so tightly to her delectable curves it might as well have been invisible.

He hadn't given her his greatcoat out of concern for her wellbeing as much as concern for *his.* Ambrose prided himself on his ruthless control, but in that moment, sitting across from his soaking wet wife with her dusky rose nipples pressing against damp fabric . . . he'd been close to losing it. Closer than he'd ever been before.

And that was . . . unsettling.

Even more unsettling than learning she still fully intended to go forward with her outrageous plan to take a lover in London.

Mara, in the arms of another man?

He struggled to picture her in *his* arms.

It was so long since last they'd touched that his memories of any intimacy shared between them were as fleeting as fog floating above a pond at sunrise. Although he did recall, with vivid clarity, their first kiss—their first real kiss. It had been raining, just like it was now. Heavy layers of water that had pounded relentlessly on the roof of the Lyceum Theater, drowning out of the voices of the actors on the stage. He had been seated beside Mara high up in a balcony box, and while she'd watched *Hamlet*, he'd watched her.

She'd worn a drab gown of gray, and whatever lady's maid had taken great pain to slick every auburn curl to her head with pomade deserved to be dismissed. Her only jewelry was a pair of small pearl earrings. Her throat was bare, her wrists as well, and he'd taken a mental note to have a sapphire choker and matching bracelet delivered to her doorstep the next morning. The rich blue would complement her ivory skin in a way that all of that dour gray did not.

As a dramatic scene unfolded across center stage, her eyes had widened. Drenched in candlelight, her irises were a shade lighter than they'd appeared at the ball. Amber, almost, with flecks of gold. He found them to be almost her most intriguing feature, second only to the light spattering of freckles across the bridge of her nose.

Ambrose had never fancied himself as a man that even noticed such minute details on a woman, let alone took a liking to them. Breasts, bottoms, calves, even the slender curve of an exposed shoulder was worth a whistle of appreciation. But with the way that Mara dressed, all of those body parts were covered and then some, leaving him with her face . . . and her freckles.

He'd wondered if she had freckles elsewhere and was mildly surprised that he genuinely wanted to find out the answer. Lady Marabelle Holden was not his guest that evening due to any sort of desire or attraction, but rather for the simple fact that she possessed nearly all of the qualities he was seeking in a duchess.

She was biddable, quiet, and came from a family of decent lineage. His solicitor had been unable to find a whiff of scandal attached to her name, and she was, presumably, a virgin. Not that he'd really cared one way or the other (the more experience in the bedroom the better, in his mind), but he didn't want any doubt cast upon the parentage of his future son and heir.

He'd also liked that she appeared organized and studious; two qualities that were often overlooked but quite necessary if a wife was to manage a household without constantly turning to her husband to solve problems. Because after he planted a babe in his future duchess's womb, Ambrose didn't want her turning to him at all. Not out of bed . . . nor in it. Their lives, for all intents and purposes, would be completely separate. She would remain primarily at Southwick Castle, while he maintained a permanent residence at Glendale Manor. An unconventional requirement that was, for him, non-negotiable.

Thus far, his search for a wife had yielded women that were either too stutteringly shy or too incessantly chatty. He'd met a blonde that he had to physically pry off his arm, and a brunette whose eyes had glazed over when he broached the subject of estate management. But Mara . . . Mara was seemingly perfect.

Except for those damned freckles.

He hadn't liked their power to distract him. He'd always enjoyed the theater, and this acting troupe in particular. But instead of his gaze remaining on the stage where it belonged, it had kept wandering to his right where Mara sat, hands folded demurely in her lap, pure and utter enchantment scrawled across every inch of her face . . . including the miniature specks of gold dust sprinkled high on her cheeks as if put there by fairies.

After the play had concluded and the actors had taken their

final bows to a roar of applause, Ambrose had escorted Mara and her sister—whose countenance, while beautiful, did not sport a single freckle—out of the Lyceum via a private exit and immediately into his carriage before the throngs of curious onlookers and gossipmongers could descend upon them.

"What did you think?" he'd asked, a politely empty smile claiming the corners of his mouth as they pulled away from the curb, the wheels clattering over uneven cobblestone before finding purchase on a smoother stretch of freshly laid gravel.

"Too much dialogue for me," said Kitty, catching a yawn in her hand. "Talk, talk, talk. This above all, to be or not to be, be true to yourselves . . . it was all a tad boring, wasn't it?"

"I believe the lady doth protest too much," Mara had said softly.

Against his will, Ambrose's teeth flashed in a grin.

Biddable, quiet, *and* in possession of a quick wit.

Yes, she'd do.

She'd do quite nicely.

"Have you attended a showing at the Lyceum before, Lady Marabelle?" he'd asked, finding and holding her gaze in the dimly lit interior of the carriage.

"Oh, no. We've never been able to—that is, no." A curl pinged loose from her tight coiffure in a desperate bid for freedom as she shook her head from side to side. "This was the first time. It's a beautiful theater. The quality of the sound was quite remarkable despite the rain, especially during the monologues."

"I agree. It's the way they designed the ceiling above the stage. It curves up and away from the floor, carrying the sound out to the audience instead of keeping it trapped over the actors." And wasn't it rather pleasant, to discuss a topic other than the weather, or the Prince Regent's wardrobe, or the myriad of other boring subjects that seemed to fascinate most women of the *ton*?

Against his will, Ambrose had found himself looking at Mara's freckles again . . . and then lower to her lips, where the top curved over the bottom in the shape of a cupid's bow.

What would that full, slightly uneven mouth feel like pressed flush against his?

What would it taste like?

What sound would she make when he nipped that plump upper lip, then soothed the bite with his tongue before it turned into a bruise?

The rush of arousal had come upon him unexpectedly; a hard punch to the gut when he hadn't even seen the fist coming, and a reminder that since parting ways with his mistress some four months past, he'd sated his more basic desires with nothing more than a flacon of olive oil and his own hand.

Purposefully averting his gaze in an attempt to cool his ardor, he'd focused on the passing scenery for the remainder of the carriage ride, his conversation clipped and noncommittal. When they'd arrived in front of the Holden residence, a townhouse overlaid in brick tucked between two nearly identical homes, he'd departed first, discreetly adjusting the front of his trousers as he went. The downpour had slowed to a misting drizzle. It was precipitation of a sort that was so common in London it might as well have been sunshine and prompted Ambrose to remove his hat and place it under his arm before he assisted Kitty to the ground.

She had fluttered her lashes at him while he helped her navigate the narrow carriage steps, much as she'd done for the entirety of the evening. And, much as *he'd* done for the entirety of the evening, he ignored her.

At first glance, Lady Katherine Holden was precisely the type of debutante that the *ton* assumed a duke such as himself would fancy. She was fashionable, flirtatious, and stunningly gorgeous, her hair the perfect shade of blonde and her eyes as blue as the sky. But while he might have considered her for a mistress if she weren't directly related to the woman he had decided to marry, she wasn't the kind of duchess he wanted.

"Lady Marabelle, might I steal a word in private?" he had said, and at her shy, hesitant nod, Kitty flounced off to the house in a huff of poorly veiled disappointment.

"What is it, Your Grace?" she'd asked, her nerves evident as she twined her fingers together. Like him, she'd also removed her hat, and the mist was dewing her hair, forming a shimmering veil that worked rapidly to dissolve the thick layers of lacquer.

"I prefer your hair like this. Soft and damp, with the ends turning into curls," he'd said gruffly, the admission spilling forth without calculation or plan, causing his brow to furrow. A furrow that turned into a tense line when he reached out and caught a tendril, rubbing it between the pad of his thumb and index finger. A gentle pull and she stepped toward him automatically, a wide-eyed filly just introduced to the halter. And he held the lead.

"Your Grace?" She bit her bottom lip then, and it was all he could do not to groan. "What—what are you doing?"

What the devil *was* he doing? Besides imagining pressing Mara up against the iron gate behind her, pinning her slender wrists above her head, and using his tongue to—

"Nothing," he'd snapped, dropping her hair as if it suddenly turned to fire in his fingers. "I'm not doing anything."

Certainly I'm not picturing you naked, your nipples taut and pointed to the sky as I hold your hips against cold metal and lick my way up one of your warm, silken thighs.

"Oh." She released her lip with a little *pop* of suction. "Could I . . . could I go inside, then?"

"Yes. Wait." He had run an agitated hand through his hair. "Before I speak with your father, I should like to ensure that you would like to further pursue a courtship. I don't intend to waste my time if your interests lie elsewhere."

"A courtship." Her cheeks paled, causing her freckles to stand out in stark contrast. He'd counted eleven before he wrenched his gaze away. "With . . . with *you?*"

"No, with the man standing beside me." Women had attempted to woo him with feigned innocence before, but it was Mara's beguiling naivety that had summoned an exceedingly scarce smile, the fit of it tight across his mouth, like a muscle that hadn't been stretched in some time. "Yes, Lady Marabelle, a courtship with me. Is that something you would find pleasing?"

"I'm not sure." She'd looked over his shoulder, at the ground, around the carriage—anywhere and everywhere but directly at him. "I did enjoy the theater, but . . ."

"But?" He captured her chin, applying just enough pressure so that she'd *had* to look at him, her lashes as dark and thick as spilled ink above watchful, wary eyes.

"But you're a duke," she had whispered, as if it were some great secret. "I'm not sure if I'm meant to be a duchess."

"Why don't we practice," he said huskily, "and find out?"

Tilting her face back, he kissed her then as a rose petal would rest upon the water. Lightly. Softly. With nary a ripple to disturb what swam beneath.

A brush of lips. An exchange of breaths.

His, long and steady.

Hers, quick and shallow.

That was to be the end of it. A hint of what was to come, nothing more. But while his head told him to stop, his heart—that frozen ball of ice wedged in the pit of his chest—urged him to continue with a wild *thump* that caught him off guard.

Raising his other hand, he cupped her delicate jawline as he took the kiss further, tasting her gasp of surprise on the tip of his tongue. It was sweet. *She* was sweet—fresh strawberries covered in cream—and he wanted to lick the bowl clean.

Their bodies had come together, their clothes wet but the skin underneath shockingly hot. Instinctively shielding what shouldn't have been happening, not with an innocent and not with *this* innocent in particular, Ambrose had spun her around to the carriage without breaking the kiss. Now if any curious bystander peeped out their window they would see the bulk of his greatcoat and little else as his broad physique easily dwarfed Mara's sylphlike frame.

His fingers then plunged into copper coils, greedily exploring the texture of her hair while his tongue traced along the seam of her lips and then, with a broad stroke that elicited another gasp, explored inside the moist cavern of her mouth.

One stroke, two, three, before he retreated to sink his teeth into her lower lip and tugged until he heard a soft, helpless mewl spill from the depths of her throat. The sound had turned his blood to flame and his cock to marble. It throbbed against his trousers, as hard as it had ever been, a damp bead of his seed already waiting at the top.

Anchoring a fist amidst her riotous mane of curls, he'd dragged her head back and deepened the kiss in a vain effort to sate the beast that was bucking within him, snarling for release. Given free rein, the beast would have taken Mara in the carriage, pushed her against the seat, and done indescribably wicked things to her. Things that would make her scream. Things that would make her pant. Things that would make her beg.

Things that were for a mistress, not a wife.

Letting go of her hair, he'd staggered away, keeping his expression consciously blank while behind it his brain pin fired in a hundred different directions.

What the bloody hell was he doing, kissing her like that?

Kissing her like he couldn't wait to feel her slick, virgin quim tighten around his pulsing member as he slid inside of her, inch by torturously delicious inch. Kissing her like he wanted to spend an hour, a night, a *lifetime* exploring every curve, slant, and hollow of her delectable body.

When his gaze grew hooded, Ambrose was the one that looked away.

Away from Mara.

Away from the carriage he still wanted to put her in.

Away from his own secret, burning desires.

And he knew then, in that flash of unacceptable weakness, that he could never kiss her like that again. Because if he did . . . if he did, the future he had painstakingly envisioned would come crashing down around him. And with it, his control. The control that he *needed* to prevent himself from ever turning back into the small, sniveling, helpless coward of boy he'd been when he had allowed his father's heel to press on his neck.

"I'll call on you tomorrow at half past ten. Wear clothing suitable for the outdoors," he'd said, and it wasn't a question but a demand. Because that was what the Duke of Southwick did, he reminded himself. He demanded things. Of people. Of places. Of objects. And they obeyed him without fail, because *he* had his heel on *their* necks where he was able to execute ruthless, unwavering authority.

His wife would be no different.

Mara would be no different.

Another piece in his proverbial kingdom to be moved at his command.

He had waited for her to say something, but she didn't speak. Her lips parted, but no noise escaped. Instead, she'd merely stared at him with her wide, coffee-colored eyes. Then, after giving the tiniest of nods, she had turned and walked away.

CHAPTER FIVE

March 1813
Southwick Castle, Derbyshire, England

A MBROSE WAS AT Southwick Castle.
Ambrose was at Southwick *Castle*.
Ambrose was at Southwick Castle.

As Mara fled up the stairs, the train of her dress leaving a wet, slithering trail in her wake, those two things—Ambrose and Southwick Castle—seemed nearly impossible to reconcile.

For as long as she'd known him, her husband had made no secret of the loathing he harbored for his ancestral home. He'd never gone into great detail as to *why* he hated the rambling labyrinth of turrets, long twisting hallways, and towering great rooms with chandeliers made from the antlers of animals long since dead, and she'd never dared ask, not wanting to risk his ire.

It was bred into Mara's bones not to provoke a man's temper but instead to do everything in her power to keep it dormant. To remain quiet, keep her questions to herself, and tiptoe when she wanted to run.

Thus, she hadn't ever queried what it was about this estate in particular that made Ambrose's eyes frost over when it was mentioned in conversation, or why he had never shared a single story of his childhood here. She'd merely come to take it for granted that this was the one place he *wouldn't* come, and if it was to be her prison, then at least it was a prison that held her greatest adversary at bay.

Yet here he was, in the flesh, and the unfairness of it brought a flood of hot, needling tears to her eyes as she called for her maid to help her change into dry garments.

Why now, she wondered with an uncharacteristic surge of resentment that burned in her chest like acid as she raised her arms above her head and her maid, Agnes, got to work on the row of buttons that ran the length of her spine. Now, when she'd finally—finally—gathered the courage to do something about her circumstances. To do something for *herself*.

Going to London, partaking in the Season, finding a companion—it wasn't for the benefit of her father, or her sister, or her husband. It was for *her*. For Marabelle. For the frightened girl turned timid woman who had never, ever done anything with her own self-interest in mind.

She hadn't wanted *this* life. As preposterous as it sounded, the last thing she'd ever desired was to be a duchess. The acclaim, the prestige, and the attention weren't for her. Certainly *Ambrose* wasn't for her.

When she was small, hiding under her bed or in a closet or outside the rickety old shed that housed the gardening tools, she hadn't dreamt of a grand life, as Kitty had, but of a simple one. A quiet one. A happy one.

With a husband who loved her.

"Ouch," she exclaimed, wincing when Agnes's comb snagged on a wet, knotted tendril.

"Ye should dry yer hair first," the older Scottish woman said wisely. "And yer skin, besides. Yer cold tae the touch, my lady. Here's a robe for ye, and there's already a fire roaring in the blue room that'll warm ye up in a lick."

"The blue room?" A flicker of apprehension went through Mara as she threaded her arms through the soft sleeves of a silk robe and tied it firmly at her waist. The room that Agnes spoke of was a daintily furnished parlor connecting her private bedchamber with the master bedchamber. That was to say, *Ambrose's* bedchamber. The room had been vacant more than it had been occupied, but now that he was at the castle, she could only assume it was where he would be sleeping. What if he walked in and—

Stop it, she scolded herself. *This is your home as much as it is his, and you'll not be walking on eggshells in it.*

Ambrose was here, and there was nothing she could do to make him leave. But her days of cowering in the presence of men had ended with the death of her father. For all of his faults, Ambrose had never raised his voice nor his hand toward her . . . and she wouldn't cower around the castle as if he were about to start at any second.

She refused.

"Aye, my lady." Agnes's mob cap fluttered as her head bobbed up and down on a bony neck. "There's another fire in the drawing room downstairs, but I dinna—"

"The blue room shall be fine. Thank you, Agnes."

The maid curtsied. "Yer welcome, my lady."

⇒⇒⇒⇐⇐⇐

WAITING UNTIL THE duchess had left to close the door and busy herself with tidying the bed, Agnes was in the middle of stripping the pillowcases when Lucy, a young servant who worked primarily in the kitchen, entered the chamber carrying a basket of fresh linens.

"Put those on the wooden chest," Agnes directed, "and be about yer business. His Grace has just arrived, and he doesn't take kindly tae dallying."

"I've been running like a hen with her head cut off since sunup." Dropping the heavy basket where Agnes wanted it, Lucy groaned as she stretched her arms above her head. "Why did

Sarah have to pick *today* to wake up retching into a chamber pot? I can't do her duties and mine! My feet are going to fall off."

"With the way Sarah's been carrying on with that lad from the stables, I expected her tae catch the morning sickness sooner or later. Mind that ye tell her tae get herself down tae the village church and be lively about it, less people start counting the weeks after the babe has arrived," Agnes said wisely.

Lucy's arms dropped. "You think Sarah is with *child?*"

"If there isn't a wee bairn growing in that lass's belly, then I wasn't born and raised in Dunkeld."

"But that means I'll have to do even more work, and on a scullery maid's wages!"

"Aye," said Agnes without a trace of sympathy. "Take this pile of dirty linens tae the laundry and see that they're washed with the lavender soap, not the plain. The plain is for His Grace."

"What's he like?" Lucy asked as she gathered the sheets and the pillowcases. "The duke."

"Haven't ye met him?"

"No, I started after Christmas."

"That's right, I forgot ye are new. Tae begin with, His Grace hates it here. He always has, ever since he was a small lad. That means he will'na have the patience for servants that stand around gossiping when they should be attending tae their duties," Agnes said pointedly.

Hugging the used linens to her chest, Lucy ignored the thinly veiled warning. "If he hates the castle that much, then why is he here?"

Inadvertently, Agnes gaze went to the duchess's writing desk and the leatherbound journal residing within it. The journal that she'd taken to reading some months ago, for how else was she supposed to know when Her Grace required a sympathetic ear and a shoulder to lean on? Stoic as an empty wall, that one, when the pages of her journal were overflowing with words of sadness and sorrow.

At first, Agnes had stolen quick glances at paragraphs. Then pages. Soon, while the duchess took her long walks through the countryside, she was reading entire passages. And it was wrong. A terrible breach of trust, to be sure, and the fastest way to be fired short of emptying the drawers of silver. But with no family except for a sister that Agnes didn't particularly care for, who else was going to look after the duchess's best interests? Who else was going to guard her well-being? Who else was going to discover her misguided plan to take a lover in London? And who else was going to plant whispers with fellow servants in neighboring households to ensure that the news was spread far and wide, thus bringing the duke to Southwick Castle?

Agnes was eighteen years happily married to an Englishman that her parents had vehemently disapproved of. They were content and comfortable but had never been blessed with children. A miscarriage and two stillborn, after which neither had the will to try again. But they had each other, they had the castle, and they had the duke and duchess, the latter of which Agnes had taken firmly under her wing whether she was aware of it or not.

It was a servant's place to tend the household, not the people that owned it. But what was a household without a heart, and whom did the heart belong to if not the master and his lady wife?

The duke likely did not remember the treats that she'd snuck him when he was a boy and she a mere scullery maid like that lazy Lucy, but Agnes did. She also remembered when the duke's father had closed his study door with the young duke inside and the crack of a birch rod that had soon followed.

She remembered when the duke stopped taking her chocolates.

When he became solemn and stern.

When his smile turned into a perpetual frown.

And she remembered the hope that had stirred in her breast when he'd returned to Southwick Castle to present his duchess, a lady as sweet and quiet as a lamb. Mara was everything that she'd ever wanted for the duke. Mara was everything that he *deserved* after all he'd been made to suffer at the hands of a father that had turned a kind, inquisitive, gentle boy into a cold, arrogant, unfeeling man.

But not cruel.

The duke didn't have the streak of cruelty that his sire had possessed, and Agnes was thankful for small acts of grace. But how she yearned to take him by the shoulders and give him a solid shake! To march him right up to his lonely, lovely wife and show him what he was missing. What he was choosing to purposefully forsake.

Of course she wouldn't do *that*. Not if she valued her position and her livelihood, which she did, very much. But she could read a journal. And she could spread a rumor. And she could bring the duke to his duchess.

The rest . . .

The rest would have to be up to them.

CHAPTER SIX

R AIN LASHED AT the windows as Mara entered the blue room
and went straight to the stone hearth where a fire crackled
merrily, just as Agnes had promised. Dragging a footstool across
the carpet, she sat down in front of it and draped her hair across
the velvet cushioning to dry, not unlike the maids hanging sheets
in the sunshine. Then she closed her eyes and forced herself to
take three deep, even breaths.

From the other side of the door connecting the blue room to
her bedroom she heard the quiet hum of voices, indicating that
Agnes had been joined by another servant. From the door that led
directly to the duke's private chamber she heard nothing . . . and
she was grateful for the silence.

Maybe it meant that Ambrose was already on his way back to
London, and wouldn't that be a relief? Not so long ago she'd sat
in this very parlor and wished away the hours until he visited her
again. But that was then, when she had been a naïve bride, and
this was now, when she'd become a disillusioned wife. A wife
who wanted nothing to do with the husband who had used her
and then abandoned her as if she were of no more consequence
than a cloak gone out of style and relegated to the back of the
closet with the rest of the unwanted garments.

How *dare* he assume that he could come here, snap his fingers, and she would trot to heel! Whatever rumors had spread of her planned misdeeds weren't her fault, as she truly hadn't told a soul. But it didn't matter if the *ton* knew or not. She was done playing the part of dutiful duchess for a duke who didn't want her! And she'd rather chew off her own tongue than accompany him to London.

When she went, she would go alone. There'd be no mutual outings, no public appearances of commitment, and she'd *not* pretend to fall ill. This was her time to do what she wanted with whom she wanted.

Ambrose . . . Ambrose be damned!

The creak of a door's hinges had Mara lifting her head, but it wasn't the door to her bedroom that opened.

"What—what are you doing in here?" she sputtered, bolting upright and wrapping her arms around herself when her husband strolled languidly into the room.

He'd changed out of his traveling clothes and into a pair of straight black trousers and a white shirt that wasn't yet buttoned to the throat. His satin waistcoat hung open and a cravat was tossed carelessly over his shoulder, a sign that he was in the midst of getting dressed. But even with his attire halfway complete, he was twice as handsome as any gentleman she'd ever met, and Mara swallowed convulsively when he took a step toward her, his glittering gaze unreadable in the firelight.

"I'm searching for my pair of gold cufflinks," he said. "My valet, disorganized fellow that he is, seems to be under the impression that they may be in here."

"Well, they're not," she said without bothering to take even a cursory glance around the parlor. "So you can leave."

"Maybe I've found something better than cufflinks."

"What's—what's that?"

A wolf's smile cut into the corners of his mouth as he prowled even closer, trailing his fingers along the rigid back of a sofa. "My wife in nothing more than a dressing robe."

Why is he looking at me like that, she wondered frantically.

He had *never* looked at her like that.

As if she were an object to be coveted. Or a dessert to be craved, one spoonful at a time.

"You should leave," she said, and her pulse kicked like a hare when, instead of exiting the room as she'd requested, he moved closer, his bare feet gliding soundlessly across the floor.

"It occurred to me that I should ask you," he murmured, raking his piercing blue eyes across her and then *through* her, as if he were privy to every inch of naked flesh underneath her robe . . . and he liked what he saw.

"Ask—ask me what?" Working feverishly, she tied another knot in the sash around the waist and then folded her arms across her chest for good measure in an attempt to guard herself from the scorching heat of his relentless gaze. Outside the cozy confines of the blue room, the storm raged on. The wind howled. The rain pounded. But inside, one could have heard a pin drop as the Duke of Southwick approached his duchess and lifted a russet curl off her shoulder.

His nostrils flaring, he leaned in close, and she froze like a deer in the crosshairs of a hunter's rifle when his words flowed across her skin like fingertips. "Why do you want a lover in London when you've a lover right here, at Southwick Castle?"

"Because—because I don't have a lover here," she said haltingly, staring straight past him at a painting on the wall as every fiber of her being screamed at her to run. Except for trickle of dampness between her thighs that ordered her to stay.

Mara was not immune to the calls of desire, and how unfair it was that Ambrose was choosing *now* to lure her in! She knew him well enough to be cognizant of the fact that he didn't want her any more than he had yesterday, or the day before that, or the day before that. He merely didn't want anyone *else* to want her. Like a dragon guarding its treasures, he preferred her to remain locked away in a cave, hidden from those who would appreciate her shine.

She flinched when he stepped around behind her, the muscles

in her abdomen quivering. Gliding his hand through her hair—despite his indifference to every other part of her, he'd always appeared strangely fascinated by her hair, as if the tumble of tendrils and tresses were a puzzle that he wanted to spend hours solving—he swept the heavy mass of it away from her neck and replaced the curls with his mouth.

"Ambrose, what . . . what are you doing?" She hated that her voice was weak. Hated that her resolve to resist him was even weaker.

Hadn't she learned her lesson?

She knew where these sweet kisses led.

First to heaven, and then straight to hell.

"Tasting you," he said simply before his teeth clasped on her earlobe and he gave a light, teasing tug that had her sagging helplessly against him, her head lolling onto his shoulder as he reached around and cupped her breast.

Circling her nipple with the rough pad of his thumb, he continued his assault on her defenses with a trail of kisses that ran the length of her neck and ended at the groove above her clavicle. When his tongue dipped into the sensitive hollow she closed her eyes, shamefully surrendering to the inevitable truth that she'd never been able to deny Ambrose and she never *would* be able to deny Ambrose.

Loving him wasn't the problem.

Her weak, foolish heart had belonged to him since the night of the Glendale Ball.

But *being* loved by Ambrose—having her feelings reciprocated and returned—therein laid the root of all her hurt.

Thunder boomed and lightning lit the sky in a zigzag of white as the early spring tempest intensified. Splaying his hand across her belly, Ambrose pulled her in taut against his powerful frame and her heart leapt when she felt the full, potent strength of his arousal jutting proudly at the small of her back.

On their wedding night, the sheer *size* of him had made her feel dizzy and that was even before their failed attempt at copulation. Courtesy of anatomy books and Kitty's superior knowledge, she'd been aware of what a man looked like down there. But what she *hadn't* been aware of was Ambrose's length and girth. Too wide to wrap her hand around, and when he'd tried to place it inside of her . . . suffice it to say there were tears shed, and while she wasn't absolutely certain on the qualifying parameters, she was fairly sure that she remained a virgin wife.

She'd let her fear get the best of her. Fear that had made her stiff and inflexible. Fear that had left her frozen.

Just lay there and let him do what he wants, Kitty had advised in the days leading up to the wedding, and Mara had tried. She truly had. But it hadn't worked. None of it. And in the end, Ambrose had left the bedchamber with a growl of dissatisfaction, and he hadn't come back.

Ever.

But he was here now, along with his enormous . . . *arousal.*

And instead of being fearful, Mara was a duchess on fire.

On a gasp, her head dropped back onto his shoulder as his hand dipped between her legs. He stroked her gently, soft, feathery-like passes of his fingertips over the thin layer of silk that covered her most intimate cove. All the while he kept kissing her, his mouth a fiery brand across her neck, her collarbone, her ear, anywhere and everywhere that he was capable of reaching.

"Do you like when I pet you?" he asked in a husky, vibrating whisper that made her toes curl. "Spread your thighs for me, Mara. Yes. Just like that. Good girl."

He untied the knots that bound her robe closed with ease and the garment fell open, bathing her skin in flickering firelight from the rosy tips of her nipples to the thatch of russet below her belly. Bringing a finger to her lips, he danced it lightly across the seam before she understood what he was asking and hesitantly opened for him.

Feeling embarrassed yet oddly excited, she wet his digit with her tongue, swirling the tip across the nail and each knuckle. He tasted of salt and sin, and when he removed his finger and immediately put it on the damp, aching pearl at the juncture of her thighs, her cheeks burned red and then redder still as he began to draw small, teasing circles.

Pleasure came on in a hazy wave as she found herself engulfed by him . . . his mouth at her nape, his left hand at her breast, and his right at the pulsing center of all her desire.

"You're wet for me," he said, and the distinct note of approval in his tone brought on a flush of gratification, not unlike the kind she'd experienced whenever a tutor had praised her knowledge of a certain subject. "God, Mara. You're fucking *soaked.*"

To prove his point, he took the same finger that had been inside her mouth and put it inside her down *there*. Startled, her muscles instinctively clenched around the intrusion and he groaned, his forehead dropping onto her shoulder.

"Bloody hell." His groan of breath almost felt like an admission of guilt, though she hadn't any idea what he was confessing to. She was too focused on the fireworks in her belly, each explosion of light flooding her veins with pure, unadulterated passion that had her leaning back against him, shamelessly splaying her legs as a common trollop might in an alley for a coin. Except it wasn't money that Mara craved. No, what she wanted was far more intangible than a simple monetary transaction. What she wanted—what her supple, yearning body *demanded*—was nothing less than everything.

From Ambrose . . . and from herself.

Complete and utter surrender.

That was the price she was willing to pay.

He rolled her swollen nipple between his fingers, toying with it almost absently, as if her breasts were an afterthought whilst his other hand played between her thighs. Stroking. Patting. Circling. Coaxing her *toward* something, although she knew not what.

Then the fingers on her nipple clamped down as the finger dancing along the seam of her dampness plunged inside of her, and the unearthly combination of pain and pleasure was . . .

cataclysmic.

On a soft cry, she arched her spine away from him which only served to drive her pelvis further onto his hand. Her eyes sprang open, revealing both her surroundings and a completely unexplored realm of sated desire.

"Easy," Ambrose murmured in her ear as her body started to tremble and her knees shook, muscle and tendon that had held her sturdily her entire life giving way in a blink. "I've got you, Mara. I've got you." He wrapped his arms around her waist, holding her against the firm wall of his chest as the spinning world steadied and she found her footing.

"What . . . what *was* that, Ambrose?" she breathed, half afraid to ask but too intrigued not to.

"Your first orgasm, and I suppose I've myself to blame. Our wedding night was hardly the stuff of legend." He traced a line across her ribcage before retying her robe. "I was half drunk, and impatient, and nervous to bed a virgin."

"*You* were nervous?" she said dubiously.

His grinned into her hair. "Does that surprise you?"

This entire day surprised her.

Ambrose surprised her. At least, this version of him—a side of himself that he'd so rarely showed her. Passionate. Vulnerable.

Kind.

The husband she had once hoped to marry instead of the cold-hearted tyrant she'd ended up with.

"I was nervous, too." Spying a pitcher of water on a nearby table, she extricated herself from Ambrose's grasp and poured two glasses, but when she held one out he declined and went to the liquor cabinet instead.

"Nervous? You were shaking like a leaf." Filling the bottom of a crystal tumbler with amber brandy, he sloshed the liquid around before taking a sip and propping his rugged length against a bookshelf. His dark hair, uncharacteristically disheveled, hung low over his brow, granting him a decidedly rakish appearance as the edge of his mouth curled with amusement. "I wasn't sure whether you were going to bolt or burst into tears."

"I wanted to do both," she admitted before taking a drink of water and finding a seat on the velvet corner of a chaise lounge. The storm had quieted, thunder and lightning giving way to a steady rain. So, too, had Mara's pulse calmed, the frantic flutter settling to a steady throb as she contemplated her husband over the rim of her glass. "But my sister advised me not to move."

"Lovemaking isn't a tooth extraction," Ambrose said dryly. "You're permitted to express yourself. It's encouraged, even."

"I was frightened."

"Yes. Yes, you were. And I handled it bloody poorly." A shadow rippled across his countenance. "For that I am sorry, Mara."

And for the rest of it? She wanted to ask. *For abandoning me here. For treating me as a means to an end instead of a wife. For promising me one life and giving me another. Are you sorry for that, as well?*

She took a deep breath. "Ambrose—"

"I have considered your wish to have an affair," he said, cutting her off. "And I've decided to help you."

"Help me," she repeated blankly.

"Indeed." He tapped his finger—the same finger that had been in her—along the side of his tumbler before taking another sip. "You'll want to make certain that you pick the right partner, and I can assist you."

Mara paled. "I don't think—"

"If some cad is going to sleep with my wife, shouldn't I be part of the decision-making process?" he queried, arching a brow.

"I never said I planned to *sleep* with—"

"There's also the matter of your preparation." He clucked his tongue. "You cannot hope to attract the sort of high caliber lover that a woman of your stature deserves unless you've some tricks up your sleeve."

"Tricks," she repeated faintly.

"Our lessons will begin on the morrow." Above the affable twist of his lips, his gaze hardened. "This is the bargain I am willing to strike with you, Mara. Accept it or not. The choice is yours."

"And if I *don't* accept?"

"Then you'll accompany me to London, as we discussed, and play the part of doting wife to perfection before returning to Southwick Castle *sans* your precious lover."

"That isn't a choice!" she burst out, half-rising from her chair. "That's—that's a decree!"

Ambrose shrugged. "I'll give you the night to think it over."

How gracious of you, she thought bitterly as he quit the room . . . locking the door behind him on his way out.

CHAPTER SEVEN

The Next Morning
Southwick Castle, Derbyshire, England

W HAT HAD HE done?
Worse yet, what had he *offered?*

As it was too early for brandy, even by his standards, Ambrose requested coffee, the color of it as black as his soul, and took it in the study that had once belonged to his father.

Since the late duke's death, he'd ordered all material possessions—from the wall hangings to the furniture to the bookshelves—ripped out and replaced until nary a physical trace remained of the man that had incited pure terror and shame in a scared boy of eight. But even though the mahogany panels were gone and the rich stench of his father's favorite cigar along with them, the memories of what had occurred here remained.

Memories of a childhood that Ambrose had spent his entire adulthood trying to suppress. Memories that came upon him in a spool of unwanted images and the scathing hiss of his father's voice while he sipped his coffee and sat behind his desk as if nothing was wrong. As if when he'd crossed over the threshold from the hallway to here, he hadn't still had a momentary clench of panic in his gut. As if he hadn't temporarily stood frozen with his feet planted on the same floorboards that had once been his prison while he was yelled at and berated until tears rolled silently down his cheeks. Only then to be yelled at again, for what sort of a duke-to-be *cried*?

A weak one, or so his father had said.

A cowardly one.

A duke who was never going to amount to anything, who was never going to impress *anyone*, and why had he been cursed with this embarrassing, sniveling worm of a child when he deserved a strong, capable son?

Well, he'd shown his sire differently, Ambrose mused with deliberate indifference as old emotions threatened to boil up and over. Not only had he amassed the largest fortune in coin and land that the Buxton family had ever known, but he'd also earned the unwavering respect—and fear—of his peers. It was a wise individual who realized the Duke of Southwick was not to be trifled with, and to risk invoking his wrath was to risk their own neck.

Ambrose did not crush his enemies.

That would be a mercy.

Instead, he ruined them. In every way that they could be ruined. And then, when they wished for the equivalent of death, when they pleaded for it, he merely smiled as his father had smiled at him when Ambrose stood in this very same study and wished for the earth to swallow him whole.

He had become everything that the late duke claimed he would never be, but his success was a bitter tonic when his sire wasn't alive to see it. When he couldn't shove it down the old man's throat and watch as he choked on it.

It nagged at Ambrose that his father had died before he'd come into his own. But what nagged at him even more, what truly dug under his skin, was the fact that of every living being in England and her neighboring countries, the only person—just one—who did not respect and fear him in equal measure was his own wife.

Oh, she jumped at the sight of him. And in his arms, she trembled. But out of them . . . out of them she still planned to cuckold him in front of King and country! At least she'd said nothing to the contrary. And if he weren't so infuriated by it, by *her*, he would have been in reluctant awe of her incredible brazenness. Instead, he found himself suffering from an emotion that he hadn't experienced in years.

Uncertainty.

And in his uncertainty, he'd done the unthinkable: bargain with his own duchess. And it was a bargain she'd not yet accepted, because in a stroke of regrettable lunacy (surely there was no other explanation for it) he had given her the upper hand . . . leaving him to await her decision as if he were some sort of errant schoolboy rather than one of the most powerful dukes in a generation.

Lifting a quill pen, Ambrose spun it absently between his fingers as he contemplated his next move. Like in a game of chess, he preferred to be three or four steps ahead at all times. And that was where he'd thought he was with Mara. Yes, she'd thrown him off guard in the very beginning with her guileless brown eyes and gentle naivety, but he'd found his balance quickly enough and had enacted *his* plan of a marriage lived apart. Aside from the matter of an heir, things had been going along swimmingly. Or so he'd assumed. Little had he known that while he was advancing his knight, Mara was playing a different game entirely.

The little minx had outfoxed him, and he wasn't going to have it.

Rising from his chair, Ambrose rang for Humphrey and the loyal butler responded promptly.

"How may I be of service, Your Grace?"

"Where is my wife?"

"The duchess?"

"Have I another wife, Humphrey?"

A dull flush crept up from under the butler's impeccably

knotted tie. "No, Your Grace. You do not. I . . . I believe she remains in her bedchamber."

In bed.

After their unexpected kiss (and more) in the blue room yesterday, Ambrose would have very much liked to see Mara in bed. And leaning over the bed. And pressed against the wall. And draped over the dresser.

He hadn't been lying when he told Lord Calvern that Mara was cold as ice. While their embraces during the courtship had been warm, occasionally bordering on hot, their actual wedding night had been a lake in the middle of March after a snowstorm. She'd lain unmoving in the middle of the mattress with her eyes pinched shut and her brow furrowed, as if she were calculating difficult sums instead of enjoying the lovemaking of her husband.

Given that his experience in the bedroom was generally matched in the experience exhibited by his partner, Ambrose had found himself at somewhat of a loss as he'd attempted to coax his virgin bride to relax and return his kisses. In that loss, he'd been flooded by old familiar feelings of ineptitude and failure that had culminated in him storming from the chamber and slamming the door in his wake. A childish act that he'd regretted ever since, and he now felt better for having apologized . . . albeit belatedly.

After their failed wedding night, he'd left the next morning and had allowed four months to lapse before he paid Mara another visit.

They'd sat as strangers in the parlor, their hands clasped and their sentences short.

He'd inquired if she was liking her accommodations.

She had remarked that the weather was pleasant.

Any camaraderie, any sense of familiarity that had sparked between them before their wedding, was gone, and in its place stood a wall covered in frost-tipped thorns. A wall placed there by their mutual inability to discuss what had transpired on a night that had laid their insecurities bare.

Every month that passed, the wall grew higher.

The thorns grew sharper.

The frost spread.

Until last night, when he went looking for his missing cuff-links . . . and found his duchess in a dressing robe instead. But for all the heat that he'd coaxed out of her, and despite her wet quim closing like a vice around his fingers as she came, had she recanted her absurd plan to have an affair?

No.

No, she bloody well hadn't.

Which in turn had driven him to strike a bargain with terms even *more* absurd!

"Have Mara brought to the solarium," he ordered through clenched teeth. "My wife and I have matters to discuss."

Unaware that she had been summoned, Mara laid awake in bed as she wondered whether the events of yesterday—culminating in the explosion of passion in the blue parlor—had truly occurred or were a figment of her imagination.

She *was* lonely.

Terribly so.

And in her loneliness, she *had* conjured a few illicit . . . fantasies. But with no more than her own personal knowledge to draw from, which was admittedly limited, they'd been little more than kisses and a few caresses. Nothing—*nothing*—like what had occurred yesterday, when Ambrose had played her body like a cello, coaxing note after note of wondrous pleasure from places on her skin that she hadn't even known were capable of such . . . such *rapture*. The things he'd done with his fingers—

On a squeak, Mara drew the covers over her head and buried underneath them like an animal taking refuge in its burrow. Unfortunately, there was no hiding from the loud, unannounced arrival of her sister when Kitty threw open the door, bounced across the room, and leapt onto the bed without a care for the early hour or the privacy it implied.

"Mara! You lump, wake up," she said, shaking the covers.

"What is it?" Mara popped her head out wearing a frown. Normally she was able to tolerate Kitty's selfish antics without annoyance, but this morning she'd wanted time to herself. Time to think, and to ponder, and to consider what difference—if any— the events of yesterday had on today and the days going forward.

Ambrose had offered . . . well, he'd offered the impossible.

He would permit her to take a lover *if* that lover met his approval and *after* he'd taught her some . . . tricks. Whatever that meant.

Surely he hadn't been serious.

Of *course* he hadn't been serious.

She chewed her lip. Had he?

No, she assured herself. He hadn't. He'd been mocking her. Mocking her and her decision to do something for herself. Because if there was one thing a powerful man could not abide, it was a woman daring enough to step out of his shadow and into her own light.

"Have you any idea that the duke is here?" Kitty demanded.

"Yes," Mara said wryly. "I am aware." Scooting up against the headboard when it became apparent that her sister was in no hurry to leave, she fluffed a pillow to place behind her spine and wrapped her arms around another, hugging it tight to her chest. "He arrived yesterday."

"*Yesterday?* And you didn't think to tell me?"

"I wasn't aware that I was under any obligation to inform you of my husband's movements." Mara's comment, uncharacteristically sharp, was followed by a beat of silence . . . and then Kitty slid off the mattress and sailed to the door with her nose in the air in a dramatic display of indignation.

"I don't know what side of the bed you woke up on this morning," she sniffed, "but I suggest you try rolling over to the other. If you have need of me, I'll be in the drawing room."

"Kitty, wait. I'm sorry—" But her sister was already gone. On a sigh, Mara slid bonelessly onto her back and stared up at the canopied ceiling. For a person who habitually steered clear of turmoil, she'd certainly been placing herself right in the middle of it as of late. This wasn't how it was meant to happen. All she'd wanted was a quiet return to London and an attentive companion to spend time with. Now Kitty was cross and the *ton* was buzzing with gossip all because she'd left out a singular important factor in her calculations: Ambrose.

His appearance at Southwick Castle posed any number of problems and his awareness of her plan proved most unfortunate. He'd left her alone *this* long, she thought with a frustrated huff of breath. Why couldn't he have gone on pretending that she didn't exist for one more Season? Surely he owed her that much for all the promises he'd given her . . . and all of the lies he'd kept.

At the very beginning of their courtship—if one could call being ordered to go places and having to obey a *courtship*—she had maintained hope that the glimpse of the man she'd seen after the theater, when he'd kissed her with such care—when he'd kissed her so well—was the man she might be marrying. That the arrogance, the coldness, the aloofness was the act, a shield he put in place to guard himself from those who didn't truly know him. And she wanted to know him. She was determined to, for she refused to marry a stranger. Even if he was a duke. Even if Society thought her mad . . . though not quite as mad they thought Ambrose for considering a shy, awkward wallflower as a potential bride when he had so many better options available.

On the day after their first public outing, he had taken her into full view of High Society once again, this time around Hyde Park in a gleaming black barouche carriage with the hood tied open so that anyone who cared to could cast a curious gaze upon them.

She recalled the nervous twitch of her fingers as she'd sat beside him while Kitty, dramatically beautiful in a sapphire blue gown that had made her yellow morning dress appear dowdy in comparison, perched on the bench seat across from them.

"Everyone is staring at us," she'd remarked happily, and Mara—whose upbringing had taught her to avoid drawing attention to herself at all costs—instinctively hunched her shoulders and sank low in an attempt to become as unnoticeable as possible.

"I'd advise you to refrain from staring back," Ambrose had said, affixing his arm to the door of the carriage and idly tapping his hand along the shiny lacquer, a new invention that coated previously porous surfaces in a hard, granite-like surface impervious to the effects of weather. "Else the poor people strain their necks in an attempt to be the harbingers of gossip. I personally wouldn't care to be responsible for their pain and suffering. Would *you*, Lady Katherine?"

On the verge of waving at those strolling past like a queen addressing her peasants, Kitty had sheepishly lowered her arm. "No, I would not, Your Grace."

"I assumed as much." Cynical amusement shone in the depths of his gaze as he turned his attention to Mara. "How are you finding the day, Lady Marabelle?"

"It's pleasant," she'd responded automatically.

"But?" he'd asked, somehow sensing that she'd bitten her tongue to cleave off the rest of her answer.

Her fingers, no longer twitching, gathered a fistful of yellow cotton and squeezed. *But you're acting like you didn't kiss me senseless in the mist yesterday. But our father was already in his cups when we woke this morning, and my left sleeve is hiding a bruise in the shape of his thumb. But I have yet to figure out what I am doing here or what your interest is in me.*

"But I hope we get rain later," she said instead, not ready to share her innermost thoughts and secrets with a man she hardly knew.

"And why is that? If I recall, it rained last night. Do you recall, Lady Marabelle?" The corner of his mouth lifted slightly. "If it rained?"

She blushed. "It . . . it *did*. But the flowers need more."

He stretched his arm across the curved back of their shared seat. "Are you an expert on flowers, then?"

"An expert?" She shook her head. "No, but I do like to garden."

"What else do you like?" His voice was low, and even though they were sharing a carriage with Kitty, and a park with a hundred other members of the *ton*, it was somehow intimate, as if they were the only couple around for a hundred miles. Which was absurd, because they weren't even a couple. But when he looked at her like that—all searing intensity and unwavering focus—she wanted to be. And she also wanted . . . heaven help her, she also wanted him to kiss her again.

In the rain and after the storm.

Out in the sun and under the shade.

On a cold winter's day when the fire crackled and a steamy summer night when fireflies danced beneath the stars.

She wanted his kisses in all of the seasons that were and all of the weather that could be.

Wasn't that a revelation? To want something for the sheer, selfish *desire* of it. It almost felt wrong . . . and at the same time, wickedly right.

"I like . . ." Suddenly nervous, she had wet her lips, and then wet them again when Ambrose's eyes darkened. "I like reading and embroidery. I like playing the pianoforte. Occasionally I like to paint, although I'm not very skilled. What—what pursuits do you enjoy, Your Grace?"

Without warning, the driver of the carriage then turned them sharply to the right to prevent crashing into an elderly man who had been paying closer attention to a pair of debutantes than the crowded bridle path in front of him.

Kitty had shrieked as she slid sideways into the corner of her seat while Mara fell into Ambrose's lap. He caught her securely against his side, his arm creating a steel barricade that wrapped around her waist and held her securely while the driver regained control of the rig and pulled them safely off to the side of the road.

"Are you all right?" the duke asked, his lips moving against the rebellious curls that had escaped from her bonnet. The fan of his warm breath against her bare skin ignited a spark down low, in the secret, velvety place that Society and her governess-nanny-housekeeper (how the blessed woman had maintained all three positions, particularly with Kitty as a charge, remained a mystery to this day) had told her never to think about and *never* to touch.

But contrary to her commands, it was *all* she'd thought about late last night, and in the wee hours of the morning, when she had lain awake, her breaths growing shallower and shallower as her first true kiss replayed through her mind on a hazy loop half-drowned in sleep and the lingering dregs of newly discovered lust.

As her mind had continually crept back to Ambrose, her hand had crept under the covers to her breasts. She'd been startled to find that her nipples—twin parts of her body she'd rarely paid any attention to—were hard and protruding. Fueled by curiosity and a daunting sense of depravity, she'd lightly pinched her aroused flesh between her thumb and finger . . . and swallowed a gasp at the answering rush of sensation that spread from her breasts, to her belly, to her loins, like water being poured downhill.

Her inquisitive hand had slipped below the flat plane around her navel to the downy curls nestled at the apex of her thighs. Curls that parted easily when she searched and found the small, hidden nub that tingled pleasantly when she rubbed her fingertip in a circle on top of it.

Cheeks red with shame and arousal, breaths coming in fits and starts, she had experimented with pressure and placement while the moon stood guard, its silvery light casting a steady, unwavering beacon of twilight across the end of her narrow bed.

On the other side of the room, Kitty had snored fitfully, oblivious to her sister's secret deeds under the cover of darkness and a heavy blanket. As Mara's fingers had thrummed below her waist, her heart had thrummed above it. An odd, excited, heavy beating that had urged her wrist to rotate faster, and faster, until . . .

Heavens.

Mara didn't remember if she'd cried out, but she thought it quite possible. A verbal release to the build-up of steam inside of her. A kettle whistling at the point of boil. She *did* recall yanking her hand away from her legs and pulling a pillow over her head to muffle the sound of her rapid breathing. Breathing that gradually slowed as her muscles relaxed and sleep took her into its elusive embrace.

When dawn had come, yellow light tinged with a filter of gray, she'd lain silently in her bed counting the cracks in the plaster ceiling before Kitty had woken up and come bounding over, babbling on and on about what they might do when the duke came to call.

She shook her head, as if she could shake away the memory of the night before and the uneasy mixture of pleasure and shame that accompanied it.

"I am . . . I am unharmed," she told Ambrose then in response to his query, her voice reduced to a croak that lodged uncomfortably in her throat. She coughed to clear it, then coughed again—a startled *hem hem*—when the arm around her ribcage tightened imperceptibly, tucking into his side as easily as if he were slipping her into his pocket.

"Why don't we disembark and walk?" he asked, his low baritone a rumbling caress against her nape. "There's a path through the laurel that leads to a small stream that should be far less crowded than the main thoroughfare."

"I would like to—to stretch my legs," she said faintly.

"Excellent." Exiting the carriage by swinging his leg over the side, he opened the door and then offered his forearm, which she accepted after just a moment's hesitation. A little hop, a swish of her skirts, and then she was on the ground beside him, the top of her bonnet scarcely reaching the bottom of his chin.

"I guess I'll let myself out then," Kitty said loudly as Mara and Ambrose set off toward a high green hedge. "Don't worry about me."

Walking in the duke's shadow, Mara snuck a glance at him. She found it difficult to give his countenance her full attention. Like looking directly at the sun, his dark, harsh beauty was too overwhelming to take in all at once. Particularly when it was directed at *her*.

She still hadn't the slightest notion of why his interest had extended to her and not her sister or any of the other far more fetching young ladies of the *ton*, but she wasn't going to question it and she dared not question *him*. This looming giant of High Society wielded as much, if not more, influence and political power than the Prince Regent himself.

In whispers behind closed doors, she'd overheard the Duke of Southwick described as dangerous. At the time, she'd thought little of it. An exaggeration, to be sure, for how truly dangerous could a duke be? What was he going to do, stab someone to death with his quizzing glass? Then, at the ball, and later, after the theater, she'd uncovered the truth.

Ambrose wasn't dangerous.

Fish not cooked all the way through was dangerous. Sewing without a finger protector was dangerous. Drinking Kitty's lemonade was dangerous.

But the Duke of Southwick?

He was *deadly*.

He was a bolt of lightning on a clear day. A patch of thin ice on a frozen pond. St James Square after dusk.

He was everything she'd vowed to herself that she would avoid. If she took a husband, she wanted him to be safe, steady, and secure. A mild-tempered gentleman who enjoyed his paper with a cup of tea and never rode his horse faster than a leisurely trot. But instead of *that* man, that predictable, quiet, kind man, she was strolling beside the Duke of Southwick ... the same fingers she'd used to pleasure herself while envisioning his face clinging to the rich fabric of his burgundy tailcoat.

"What hobbies do you like, Your Grace?" she mustered the

courage to ask again as they followed a trail that wound along the hedgerow. Tiny brown sparrows sang amidst the woven branches and from the other side she could hear the humming trickle of the stream that Ambrose had told her about, although it was not yet visible through the towering wall of laurel.

"I've excellent aim with a pistol, a steady seat in the saddle, and, at last count, am fluent in six languages."

Her mouth curled in a bemused half-smile. "I did not inquire what hobbies you were good at, Your Grace. I asked what ones you *enjoyed*."

"Is there a difference?"

"I believe so." She stepped nimbly over a fallen branch. "I'm sure you received excellent tutelage in any manner of subjects. But what ones do you actually like doing now that you're an adult?"

The duke frowned. "Does drinking count?"

"I'm not sure. Do you enjoy it?"

"Depending on the vintage."

"Then yes, I suppose it does." The trail veered to the left and an opening appeared in the hedgerow just wide enough for one person to fit through at a time. Mara went first and Ambrose followed right after, his hand resting on the small of her back where it remained even after the path broadened out again along a babbling brook.

Heat blooming in her cheeks, she flicked a belated glance behind them. "I—I think we've accidentally left Kitty behind."

"I'm sure she'll find her way," Ambrose said, unconcerned. Bending, he picked up a small, flat rock and with a turn of his wrist sent it across the water where it skipped once, twice, three times before sinking to the bottom.

Mara's eyes widened. "How did you do that?"

"Here, I'll show you." Scouring the ground for another rock, he found one that met his specifications and then went behind Mara. Looping an arm around her waist, he pulled her in snug against the hard wall of his chest and bent his head so that his chin rested on her shoulder. "Take the rock," he murmured, pressing the stone into her palm. "Then lift your arm like this."

She moved her body accordingly, feeling for all the world as if she were a puppet . . . and Ambrose was controlling her strings. Despite their difference in height, she was amazed to find how remarkably well they fit together. Two pieces from very different puzzles clicking firmly into place. What picture did they make, a handsome duke and the shy daughter of a viscount, standing so close together on the bank of a stream? She tried to imagine it from an outsider's perspective, but she couldn't. It was far too implausible.

Implausible, but apparently not impossible, for here they stood.

He circled his fingers around her wrist, his thumb pressing on the delicate web of green and blue veins where her pulse fluttered madly. "It's in the throwing motion," he said. "You want to spin the rock sideways, so it hits the water on the flat side."

"Like this?" Focused more of the warmth radiating from his body than the slight weight in her hand, she gave an inept toss and with a little disappointing *plop*, the rock sank, well, like a rock.

Ambrose chuckled. "Here, try again."

He moved away to retrieve a replacement, this one slightly larger and smoother than the last. This time he held her elbow, guiding it out and then in as she practiced a few throwing motions. When she was satisfied that she had the hang of it, she threw the flat rock as he'd instructed and gave a gasp of audible delight when it managed a single wobbly skip across the top of the water before disappearing.

"I did it!" she said, spinning around to Ambrose.

Spinning around *into* Ambrose. He caught her easily, as if she were a feather floating in the air. One second she was blissfully weightless. The next, held in arms of iron.

Then the iron softened . . . and he kissed her.

It wasn't the hot, heady kiss she'd received on her doorstep when he'd placed his tongue inside her mouth and she'd feared that she'd be engulfed by flame. If that kiss—her first kiss—had been a blistering August day in the height of summer, then this kiss was a cozy morning in the middle of September.

It was tea perfectly warmed with a side of cinnamon biscuits and a splash of cream. It was sweetness, and it was comfort, and it was . . . it was *safety*. Something she'd sadly known far too little of.

With her chin perched on Ambrose's finger, her lashes fanning across her cheeks and her lips pressed against his, she felt *safe*. Protected. Shielded from all of the considerable ills that awaited her at home. And how ironic that up until now neither his handsomeness, nor his title, nor his obscene wealth had convinced her he might be a wise choice for a husband . . . but this, this kiss that was infinitely more than a kiss, did.

Exhaling, he drew his head back, but when she opened her eyes she found him staring at her with an emotion she'd secretly wondered if the notoriously hard-hearted Duke of Southwick was even capable of swirling in the depths of his startlingly blue irises.

Tenderness.

He was gazing at her with such tenderness that her eyes pricked with tears, and she had to quickly glance away lest he think her foolish or given to fits of flamboyance.

"We should . . . we should search for Kitty," she said, shifting her weight from side to side. "I wouldn't want her to become lost."

"Isn't your sister meant to be chaperoning *you?*" Ambrose inquired with a devilish arch of his dark brow.

Mara had the good grace to blush. "Kitty is more accustomed to being looked after than being the one doing the looking. This is rather new territory for her."

"A common trait amidst younger siblings, I suppose. When did your mother pass?" he asked, watching her closely. It was the first time that the duke had broached such a sensitive, intimate subject, and her initial instinct was to deflect his query with a change of subject. But if they were to be married (something she was seriously considering after that kiss), wasn't that the point of having a husband? A steadfast partner to share your innermost doubts and insecurities with. A safe harbor that contained all of your secrets, even those you wanted to hide from yourself.

"My mother was . . . my mother *died* when I was twelve and Kitty ten."

"I'm sorry." He reached for her hand and ran his thumb across her knuckles. An absent gesture of affection that had her blinking the sting from her eyes. "That must have been difficult, to lose her at such a young age. Was she ill?"

The shout of voices. Her father's deep and booming. Her mother's shrill and high-pitched.

"Be quiet!" Elizabeth had cried. "You'll wake the children."

But Mara and Kitty, huddled under the same blanket in their room, were the least of Eriam's concerns on that awful, terrible, deadly night.

The sound of cursing.

Of doors slamming.

Of furniture splintering.

The race of footsteps, light and quick, on the steps . . . followed by the heavy stomp of drunken boots.

More yelling.

Mara covered her sister's ears.

She closed her eyes.

But she couldn't block out the screaming.

The fighting.

Then a single scream.

Just one.

A scream that ended in the middle where no scream should end. Cut off, like a snipped thread. And a thump, thump, thump, THUMP as something—someone—fell down the stairs.

"Stay here," Mara had whispered to Kitty. "Don't move, no matter what."

On the quietest tiptoes she went out into the hall and peered over the railing to the foyer below. Saw a crumple of purple on the floorboards. Her mother, sleeping. What a strange place to take a nap, but it was the only reality that Mara's mind would entertain. Her mother was resting. Or perhaps she'd fainted. But it was nothing worse than that. It was nothing more permanent than that. Except there was too much red. An entire puddle of it that spread to another puddle, and another. A lake's worth of red. Reaching all the way to the rug, and that was how she knew her mother was dead. Elizabeth could not abide a stain and were she able, were she breathing, she would have rushed for the nearest bucket and filled it with sudsy water. But she didn't move. Not a finger. Not a foot. Nothing stirred. Nothing jerked or trembled or flopped.

The viscountess was dead.

The viscount had killed her.

And Mara . . . Mara had paid witness to it.

"No, my mother wasn't ill." But before she could decide if she wanted to say more, if her tongue, heavy in her mouth, would *allow* her to say more, Kitty, red faced and cross, stumbled upon them.

"*There* you are," she said, glaring. "Why didn't you wait for me? Don't you know better than to run off? What if you were found alone? That would reflect poorly on me! I'm your chaperone, Mara, and—"

"Lady Marabelle was in excellent hands," Ambrose interceded smoothly, his double entendre bringing a prickle of heat to the secret garden between Mara's thighs that she was forbidden to think about. "But the morning hour is growing late, and I should probably return both of you to your father before he starts to worry."

Situated as he was beside Mara, the duke missed her instinctive flinch. But Kitty saw it, and she gave a fast, hard shake of her chin. A silent warning not to speak of the troubles that plagued them at home. To *never* speak of them. To anyone.

A suitor might overlook their small dowries, but Society would hardly permit him to marry the daughter of a murderer. Even the *hint* of such a scandal would be enough to ruin them and any future prospects they might have. And without future prospects, how were they ever to escape their past?

Pinching her lips firmly together, Mara gave a tiny nod back.

An acknowledgment that she hadn't said anything. That she *wouldn't* say anything. Because even if she did marry Ambrose, there was always divorce. A nearly unthinkable sin, and a herculean act of Parliament, but if he were to prove fraud . . .

No, she'd keep her secrets.

Carry them to the grave, if she had to.

For death with a secret was better than divorce in a society that had the ability to slice a woman to the bone even without spilling a drop of blood.

CHAPTER EIGHT

W ITH EACH MINUTE that passed and Mara did not appear, Ambrose's impatience grew. What the devil was she doing? What could possibly be more important than the husband she hadn't seen for the better part of twelve months?

His fault, he admitted.

He was the party that had stayed away, while Mara had remained right where he'd left her.

But he was here now, wasn't he?

Waiting and watching the damned clock tick, and *that* wasn't a pleasant feeling. To know that he was falling second best to whatever person or activity was preventing his wife from answering his summons. But before he was able to dwell on the uncomfortable idea that what he was experiencing now was a one-thousandth of what Mara had felt over the past year, the solarium doors opened and his duchess, fresh as a daisy in a gown of flower yellow with her hair in a tumble of auburn curls, walked in, temporarily rendering Ambrose speechless.

He'd seen her yesterday in the rain. Last night in the shadows.

Pretty both times. Pretty enough to take him aback as he'd tried to pinpoint precisely what had changed between the wife he'd left and the one he'd returned to.

But this morning, drenched in sunlight . . . she was beauty personified. And he was the fucking fool who had offered to help find her a lover because he wasn't about to be the first one in this broken farce of a union who confessed to a tangled web of emotions he'd never wanted and had absolutely no idea what to do with.

Bargains. Deals. Tit for tat.

That he understood. *That* he was good at.

As for the rest? As for the heart of a marriage?

He hadn't a bloody clue.

"There's breakfast on the sideboard," he said curtly.

She glanced at the platters of food covered in shiny silver domes. "I am not hungry."

Good, neither was he.

That meant they could get right down to business.

"Have you an answer for me?" he asked without preamble. When his chest felt tight, as if his valet had selected a waistcoat of a size too small, he drove the heel of his palm into the middle of his breastbone and scowled. "About what we discussed in the blue room."

"I'm aware of what you're referring to." The solarium boasted half a dozen circular tables draped in ivory linens and set with sparkling crystal. Past the tables was a wall of windows offering a clear view of the orchards, where a small army of servants moved along the straight rows, expertly pruning the apple trees to prepare them for a hearty autumn harvest. Gliding past Ambrose as if he were of no more significance than a chair, Mara stopped at the windowsill and frowned. "I should be out there helping them."

"Pruning is work for a servant, not a duchess."

"And what work *is* there here for a duchess?" She looked at him over her shoulder, and Ambrose was taken aback by the coolness in her stare and the rigidity of her spine.

The girl he'd married had been easily flustered, and he'd used to secretly enjoy making her stutter and blush. But the woman standing before him now was poised, collected, and prepared for battle, her defenses shored up while he'd slept . . . and dreamt only of her.

"From what I was told, a duchess is to manage a household," she went on. "But Southwick Castle runs itself. A duchess is to plan and execute social events, but there hasn't been so much as a dinner party here in years. A duchess is to sponsor a charity, but all of the charitable work is being done in London where you've made it clear that my appearance is most unwelcome. So do tell, Your Grace, what work *should* I be doing, if not lending an extra hand to those who could avail themselves of it?"

Your Grace, was it?

Last night, in the blue room, he'd been Ambrose. This morning, in the solarium, he was Your Grace. The difference was subtle but notable. A line being drawn in the imported French limestone under their feet.

"If you want to prune trees, then prune trees," he said dismissively. "But if you want to seek companionship outside of our marital bed, there are terms we need to discuss first."

"We don't *have* a marital bed."

"A figure of speech."

Her mouth thinned. "I do not recall discussing any of *your* illicit activities. If someone were to ask me, I couldn't list a single person or place of ill-repute that you've visited over the past fortnight, let alone the last year. Although I'm sure you've frequented your fair share. Why, then, should I have to undergo scrutiny and agree to ludicrous conditions in order to do what *I* want?"

"Because you're my wife," he growled.

"When it suits you," she shot back. "When it doesn't, I'm a forgotten inconvenience!"

Five steps.

Five steps was all it took to cross the invisible line, grab Mara by the arms, and cover her mouth with his.

His kiss in the blue room had been slow, simmering, and

designed to melt away her inhibitions.

His kiss in the solarium was fast, furious, and spurred by rage at the thought of another man touching what belonged to *him*.

If his conditions were ludicrous, then it was due to the fact that he wanted them to fail. But if he came right out and said that, then he'd have to explain why.

Why it mattered.

Why *she* mattered.

And sometimes . . . sometimes it was simply easier to taste than to talk.

After a pause that felt like an eternity, Mara returned his kiss, her fingers creeping up to clutch the lapels of his jacket as her tongue tentatively met his. He ran his fingers through her hair, sending pins scattering as fire coursed through his veins and the smell of lilacs invaded his nostrils, an intoxicating aphrodisiac that made him want to throw back his head and howl like a bloody wolf.

Lifting her effortlessly, he went to the nearest table and with a violent sweep of his arm sent the perfectly arranged crystalware crashing to the ground. Already lost in each other, in desires long denied and passions put by the wayside, neither acknowledged the sound or the mess as Ambrose laid Mara out across the table as if she were a sumptuous feast and he a man half-starved.

Eyes glazed, heart pounding, cock hard as a damned iron pike, he fell to his knees and shoved her skirts up and over her knees. "Hold these," he ordered, his voice muffled by the stocking he was in the midst of peeling off her slender calf . . . with his teeth.

Sunlight dappled her bare legs and he kissed each shimmering halo of golden light on his way to the top of her thighs where downy coils of red guarded her slick core. She tensed when he brushed his lips across her there, her little toes curling on his shoulders.

"Am-Ambrose, you—you can't do that," she protested, and in response he licked her, a groan rumbling in the depths of his throat at the sweet, tangy taste of her nectar on the tip of his tongue.

"Why not?" he asked, turning his head to kiss the inside of one quivering thigh.

"B-because . . . because . . ." Her toes uncurled. "I'm not sure, actually."

His vibrating chuckle landed directly on her clitoris and she cried out, thrusting her hips off the edge of the table as she grabbed his hair with both hands. Emboldened, he used his thumbs to spread her delicate folds apart and presumed to taste her in earnest . . . what had always been somewhat of a chore transforming into an act of pure pleasure for them both.

Listening to the sounds of her breaths, he took her to the brink again . . . and again . . . and again. Drawing away each time he heard her gasp, felt her body bow . . . before resuming what was surely God's work, for if this wasn't what an angel tasted like, then he'd happily damn himself to the devil.

When her velvety quim tightened around his tongue, he reached for the source of his own pulsing arousal and drew his cock from his trousers, the rounded tip already damp with seed. Using his mouth and hand in tandem, he brought them both to the edge. That wild, teetering, windswept edge where the sky blurred with the sea. Then with a ruthless plunge, he sent them careening over, his muffled groan captured by the drenched center of her ecstasy.

In the lull of panting breaths that immediately followed the swell of release, Ambrose maintained his hold on Mara's thighs, his fingers loathe to give up their grip of silken flesh. On the table, her arms flailed drowsily, knocking another glass to the floor as she struggled to sit up. Mindful of the broken shards of crystal and porcelain, he rose to his feet and proceeded to scoop her right up into his arms as if she were a pile of fluffy down, albeit one with bright red cheeks and dazed brown eyes instead of white and gray feathers.

"That . . . that . . ." She stopped. Licked her lips. "I quite enjoyed that."

"Should we make a new hobby of it?" he asked, vaguely re-calling a conversation they'd had in the park when they were courting and he taught her how to skip a rock across the water. When he'd wanted a wife who would be easy to control. A wife who wouldn't provoke any emotional response. A wife he would never love, because if there was one lesson his father had instilled in him above all others, it was that to love something was to risk the devastation that came from losing it.

"Maybe?" Mara's head fell onto his shoulder as she peeked at him from beneath her lashes. "Although a location without so much breakable dishware would probably be preferable," she said with enough seriousness that the corners of his mouth twitched. "That was a very fine set of crystal. A wedding present from the Duke of Ashcroft, I think."

Ambrose snorted. "Ashcroft is a stingy old miser. I'd be will-ing to bet a hundred pounds that's glass, not crystal, and I . . ." His mouth hung open, no sound emerging as he watched a beam of light from a nearby window dance across the dusting of freckles on her nose. "I . . ."

I am falling in love with you.

I am in love with you.

I've been in love with you.

Bloody fucking hell.

Those thoughts didn't belong in his head. They didn't belong anywhere.

Because he wasn't, and he didn't, and he couldn't.

"Ambrose?" she said, a line of uncertainty hovering above her brow. "What's wrong?"

What was wrong? What was *right*?

He'd come here with the express purpose of bringing Mara to heel whilst dispelling any fanciful ideas she might have had about taking a lover. Instead, he found himself holding her in his arms as the taste of her slowly faded from his lips and his heart hammered like that of a lovesick schoolboy.

If the late Duke of Southwick could see him now, how he would laugh. How he would ridicule. How he would *scorn*. And Ambrose, whose entire adult life had been built around the premise of making absolutely certain that his father—alive or dead—would never be able to find a sliver of vulnerability where he could stab his knife, felt his gut tighten.

"I have a correspondence that requires my attention," he said coolly before placing Mara on the ground and purposefully taking a step away from her. "Have a servant pick this mess up before someone injures themselves."

"*Ambrose.*" Bewilderment flashed in her gaze. "What—"

"That was our first lesson. Tomorrow, if I've time, we can review potential candidates."

"Lessons? Candidates?" She bit her lip. "I don't . . . oh. I understand."

No, she didn't. How could she?

How could she know that he'd rather she hate him than love him? Even though there was a part of him, a part of the boy he'd been, that desperately, desperately wanted her love. That *needed* it. A part that wanted him to lay his head upon her breast and unburden himself of all the painful secrets he kept hidden away inside. The secret of Wags, and the secret of the governess who had gently kissed his brow each night and wished him sweet dreams before his father sent her to a different household, and the secret of waiting outside his mother's door for hours with a bouquet of wilted flowers he'd picked just for her clenched in his little fist. When she had finally emerged, she'd merely gazed at the blooms in disgust and asked why he'd brought her weeds before calling for his new governess to take him to the nursery.

Everything and everyone he'd ever cared about had been lost to him.

His presence was poison.

His love was pestilence.

Sending Mara to Southwick Castle hadn't been a banishment. He'd been doing her a *favor*. Because she was better off without him. Better off *away* from him.

If he truly loved her, then he couldn't keep her.

If he truly loved her . . . then he had to let her go.

"I'll be busy for the remainder of the day," he said curtly, not quite meeting her gaze. "You will meet me for dinner at six o'clock." He began to walk toward the door. "Do not be tardy."

"Yes, Your Grace."

Ambrose hesitated, his father's voice ringing his ears. *Follow the rules I've set forth or suffer the consequences.* Grinding his teeth together, he left the solarium without looking back.

➤➤➤❖❮❮❮

WAITING UNTIL AMBROSE had gone, Mara knelt and began to gather the broken shards of crystal. She might as well have been picking up pieces of herself, for she felt as shattered as the dishware scattered across the floor.

It would have been better if he'd been cruel to her from the beginning. Then she might have worn better armor. But his earnest passion had lowered her defenses . . . right before his sword had pierced her heart.

"Why?" she asked to the empty room as she stretched her arm under a chair.

What was the point of bringing her to the highest peak only to drop her into the lowest valley? Did he derive some sort of sick pleasure from her pain? Did he *like* hurting her feelings? She didn't want to think so. But what other answer was there? None came readily to mind. Maybe he was bored and wanted a bit of sport. A dash of entertainment. But why take it at her expense? She knew—oh, how she knew—that he didn't love her, but could he hate her that much?

"Your Grace!" The shock in Agnes's voice mirrored the shock in the older woman's face as she entered the solarium and found the Duchess of Southwick crawling around the floor on her hands and knees. "What's happened? Have ye fallen? Should I have the doctor fetched?"

"No, no, I'm fine," Mara said firmly even though she was anything but. "Some glass broke, and I—"

"Ye canna pick up the mess yourself, Your Grace," Agnes protested, giving the bellpull by the door a sharp tug before she hurried over and, with a grunt of effort, dropped to her knees beside her mistress. "It's not seemly."

Leaning against the leg of a table, Mara smiled wanly at her loyal servant. "That's what my sister said when she found me pruning the rosebushes."

"In this case, Lady Katherine would be right."

"And in other cases?" Mara asked, well aware of the dismal view Agnes held of her sister.

The Scottish woman sniffed. "I couldn't say."

"I spoiled her. When we were young," Mara explained when Agnes appeared nonplussed. "Our father wasn't . . . he wasn't kind. So I endeavored to make up for his lack of kindness by showering Kitty in attention, and compliments, and treats whenever I happened to come across them. I wanted her to feel special, but now that we're grown, I fear that I may have made her feel entitled to such treatment instead. But she isn't a bad person."

Agnes's expression remained carefully stoic, her true thoughts hidden behind the laugh lines and wrinkles that time and a long, twisting journey through life had wrought. "I'd never imply that Lady Katherine is a bad person, Your Grace."

"But . . .?"

Agnes pursed her lips. "But she'd do well to adopt some of your finer qualities."

Mara gave a clipped, incredulous laugh. "And what have my so-called finer qualities got me? Sitting here, on this floor, collecting shards of crystal. Maybe I'd rather be Kitty, flitting about without a care in the world."

"If yer sister doesn't have any cares, it's because ye took them from her." Agnes patted Mara's knee. "It was sweet tae look after yer sister. Not many would have done as ye did. As ye continue tae do. But there comes a time when too much help becomes a hindrance."

"Yes." Mara huffed out a long breath of air. "I suppose you're right."

"If I had tae guess, though, I'd say that ye aren't sitting here due tae Lady Katherine."

"Your guess would be correct," she said, unable to prevent the bitterness from creeping into her tone. "You know my husband as well as anyone, Agnes. Why did he marry me?"

The servant blinked. "For sure that's a question that can only be answered by His Grace."

"But I'm asking you. Please," Mara said pleadingly, placing her hand on top of Agnes's and giving a desperate squeeze. "I know it's beyond your purview, but I also know that you've worked in this household since Ambrose was a boy."

"Ye are his wife—"

"I'm a stranger. He's a stranger. We're strangers. *Please*, Agnes. Anything you can tell me about him. Anything at all. I want . . ." She choked back a rush of tears. "I don't know what I want. But it isn't this." She looked at the small pile she'd made out of broken pieces of glass. "It *can't* be this."

Agnes softened. "I canna betray his confidence, Your Grace. Some things canna be shared but by those who went through them. But I will say . . . I will say that ye were fortunate tae have your sister. As ye are no doubt aware, the duke is an only child. And being the only one of something is an invitation tae loneliness."

A flicker of emotion passed through the servant's gaze. Later, when Mara had the time and distance to reflect upon what she'd been told, she would recognize it for what it was: pure, unadulterated hate.

"When he was a boy, His Grace found a dog. Or the dog found him. Regardless, he was wise enough tae keep it a secret, as neither of his parents had a care for pets of any kind. And the staff kept it a secret, those who knew, because we had a deep caring for the duke, well, the heir to the dukedom, as he was still in those days." Agnes's bosom heaved as she drew a ragged breath. "On the day that the late duke uncovered what his son had been hiding, he had the dog killed."

Agnes spoke so calmly, so matter-of-factly, that it took Mara a moment to digest the barbarity of her words. She stiffened, her eyes widening in horror, when they sank in. "Ambrose's father had . . . had the poor dog *killed?*"

She pictured her husband as a boy. Somber and serious, with a tousle of messy black hair and big blue eyes. A boy that laughed as a dog nipped at his heels and then licked his face. A boy devastated by the loss of his beloved pet.

"Aye, and what's worse, he made sure that His Grace understood it was his fault."

"But it wasn't!" Mara protested, anger curdling in her belly. "It wasn't his fault at all."

"Ye aren't wrong," Agnes agreed. "But a child believes what their parent tells them, and if His Grace ever began tae believe anything else, his father used a rod tae sort him out."

Unconsciously, Mara's hand drifted to her arm where her own bruises had blossomed most often, to the place where her father had always grabbed her first. A secret, ugly garden of black and blue. "Ambrose has never really spoken about his parents," she said softly. "I . . . I had no idea he was subject to such abuse."

That we both were.

The horrible irony wasn't lost on her.

The one thing they had in common—she, the simple daughter of a viscount and he, the powerful son of a duke—was the one thing they'd spent their entire marriage hiding from each other. Had she been aware of their shared past, would she have acted differently? She would have had more empathy, perhaps. Granted him more grace. Not that it would have made much of a difference, with her trapped here and him in London. Maybe no matter what, this was the end they were always destined for. That their mutual upbringings had designed them for.

Hurt and heartache.

Loneliness and loss.

What hope did they have for better?

"Please apologize on my behalf to the maids for the mess." Rising to her feet, she held out her hand to help Agnes, and the older woman gratefully accepted the assistance. "I should go and find Kitty. We exchanged cross words this morning, and I don't want them to fester." She stared at the table devoid of crystal, its linens wrinkled from her writhing body. "I won't tell Ambrose what you told me. No doubt you've heard of the rumors circulating with regard to my ... my plan for the upcoming Season."

"In a house as big as Southwick Castle I hear plenty of rumors, Your Grace, and I'm old enough tae not pay them any heed." Agnes smoothed her apron. "As for the glass, don't ye worry. Nothing's so broken that it can't be mended. Or least tidied up."

Mara managed a wobbly smile. "Are you sure?"

"Aye, that I am." She pointed at the door with a bony finger. "The last I saw of Lady Katherine, she was headed for the music room."

"Then that's where I'll start my search. Thank you, Agnes." Mara paused. "For everything."

The Scotswoman curtsied. "No trouble at all, Your Grace. No trouble at all."

CHAPTER NINE

A FTER AN EXTENSIVE search of the music room, drawing room, front parlor, and side parlor, Mara stumbled across Kitty in the ballroom, of all places. Humming a waltz, her sister was spinning across the polished wooden floorboards with her arms extended and her eyes closed, a dreamy smile capturing her lips as she danced sans partner.

Her sister truly was beautiful, Mara thought with a rare twinge of envy. In a way that she, with her curly red hair and plain brown eyes, never would be. It was Kitty who should have married a duke, and she herself would surely have found contentment with a doctor, or a solicitor, or a tradesman. But here they were, for better or worse, and not wanting to interrupt her sister, but also keen to clear any unhappiness between them, she waited along the wall for Kitty to finish.

"I can feel you staring at me," Kitty called out before her eyes popped open and she stopped in the middle of the floor with her hands on her hips. "What do you want, Mara? I'm practicing my spins."

"You needn't practice, they're already perfect."

"Maybe I want to practice. What else is there to do here?"

My point exactly, Mara thought silently. She went to a chair that a servant had likely been using as a stool to reach the cobwebs on the chandeliers and sat. What a waste this room was. Surely its original architect—the person who had poured their heart and soul into the creation of the castle—had never intended for it to sit vacant for as long as it had, collecting dust while the years passed it by. And wasn't that how *she* felt? Just like this ballroom was meant for dancing and hosting grand events, surely she was meant for more things than slowly withering away in a tomb of wood and marble.

"You ran off this morning before we could make amends," she commented, propping her chin on the heel of her palm. "My husband is already perpetually cross with me." *To put it mildly.* "I don't want my sister to be, as well."

Kitty rolled her eyes. "Not everyone is going to adore you for every hour of every day."

No, but I'd settle for a minute here or there.

"I should have told you that Ambrose had arrived. I apologize for my oversight."

"It's all right," Kitty said airily. "I forgive you." With no other chairs available, she plopped down right in the middle of the floor and brought her knees to her chest. "Is he aware? Of what you plan to do in London."

Mara laughed. It was not a happy sound. "Oh, he's aware. More than that, he's encouraging of it."

"You're jesting."

"Tomorrow we're to review a list of potential candidates."

"Now I *know* you're jesting."

"If only I were."

"He's not going to try to stop you?"

"On the contrary, he wants to give me lessons."

"In what?"

Her cheeks heated. "In . . . seduction."

"Your *husband* is going to give you *lessons* in how to seduce another man?"

"When you put it like that—"

"What other way is there to put it?" Kitty said incredulously.

"I'm not sure." As a headache settled between Mara's eyes and began to throb, she massaged the bridge of her nose. "To be completely honest, I'm not sure about anything. This is not what I wanted when I accepted Ambrose's proposal. I didn't *want* to be left here. I didn't *want* to be lonely. I didn't *want* to be married to someone who doesn't want me. But all of those things have come to pass, and I can either remain here wallowing in my self-pity, or I can do something about it. At least Ambrose is offering to be a help instead of a hindrance," she said, attempting to see the sun through the clouds. "I should be grateful."

"You *should* be checking your tea for arsenic!"

A sliver of amusement cut through the pounding in her temple. "You've been reading too many of those gothic novels. Ambrose is many things, but he's not a murderer."

"*I'll* tell you what he's not." Kitty slapped her hand on the floor. "He's not a cuckold. If you believe otherwise, then you're more a fool than he is for not recognizing how wonderful you are."

"Kitty," she exclaimed, oddly touched. "That's . . . that's the nicest thing you've ever said to me."

"Don't let it go to your head." Clambering to her feet, Kitty smoothed out her skirts and resumed her waltz position. "You need to fix whatever is broken between you and the duke before the Season begins. Have an affair, don't have an affair. But for the love of God, be discreet about it like a normal couple. We cannot afford another scandal."

"*Another* scandal?" said Mara, confused. "We haven't one now."

"We're about to."

"If you're referring to the rumors—"

"Rumors are just rumors until there's truth behind them," Kitty interrupted as she executed a flawless spin to the right. "Lady Harmsworth and her group of old crones will have some fresh meat to sink their teeth into soon enough. But we needn't deliver them a feast on a silver platter."

Mara shook her head in bewilderment. "I have no idea what you're talking about."

In a feat of perfect balance, Kitty froze on the tips of her slippers with her arms flung out in a circle and her spine bowed inward. The only sign of exertion was the rapid rise and fall of her chest. "I'm talking about my divorce."

〉〉〉≪≪

"HUMPHREY!" Ambrose bellowed, throwing open the door to his bedchamber so that his shout could ricochet down the hall. "Dammit, Humphrey, where are you?"

"Here, Your Grace." Panting slightly, the beleaguered butler hauled himself up the final steps of the staircase and half ran, half walked the last few yards with as much dignity as he could muster. "I'm here."

"About time," Ambrose grumbled, stomping across the room to a set of windows that overlooked the western lawn. Throwing open the curtains, he glared at the unfolding sunset, taking personal offense at the breathtaking spill of colors. If they'd been able to reflect his current mood, they'd have been a canvas of grays and blacks. How irritating that the world didn't revolve around him. That his *wife* apparently no longer revolved around him.

Irritating and damned inconvenient.

"How can I be of service, Your Grace?" Humphrey remained in the doorway, as much to observe proper protocol as to protect himself. Having witnessed the duke in a mood such as this one more than once, he'd learned it was best not to get too close.

"I require . . ." Ambrose hesitated. The sad truth was, he didn't need anything. Not anything that his butler could retrieve, at any rate. But as he'd paced the length of his bedchamber, his fists coiled balls of tension and his stomach a twisted knot of unease, it had occurred to him that he hadn't anyone else he was able to genuinely rely on except for Humphrey. No one who had been by his side longer. No one who knew him better. And wasn't that a sad, sorry state of affairs? His servant—not his wife, not his friends, not his mother—was his most trusted confidant. "I require an ear."

The butler paled. "An . . . an ear, Your Grace?"

"Yes," he snapped. "Your ear, to be precise."

Humphrey covered the side of his head. "My—my ear?" he squeaked.

Ambrose cast a moody gaze over his shoulder, caught the butler's uneasy expression, and rolled his eyes. "I'm not going to cut it off, Humphrey. I merely want you to listen. I . . . I want your advice."

"My advice." All things being equal, the sudden green tinge to Humphrey's jowls indicated he might have preferred to hand over an ear. "I shall endeavor to grant you whatever you'd like, Your Grace."

"The duchess and I had a disagreement. We are having trouble with the original terms of our marriage." His brow furrowed as a belated thought occurred. "Are *you* married, Humphrey?"

The butler blinked. "Me?"

"Is there someone standing behind you?"

"No, Your Grace. And no, I am not married."

"Why not?"

"I . . . I never had the inclination."

Ambrose nodded. "Smart fellow. Wives are the burden of those who must produce a legitimate heir."

Humphrey's mouth opened. Closed.

"Speak," he ordered, taking note of the small, inconspicuous movement. Not unlike a fish on land gasping for breath.

"That's not to say I don't want a wife," the butler said slowly. "But given the demands of my duties, which I am happy and proud to fulfill, I haven't yet had the opportunity to . . . to . . ."

"I haven't all afternoon, Humphrey."

"To find a woman that I love."

Love. How Ambrose despised that word. Deep down in his bones, where his marrow resided, he loathed it.

For his entire childhood, he'd chased after it. For his entire adulthood, he'd run away from it.

Now here he was, seeking counsel from his *butler.*

Where had it all gone wrong?

When you decided that it was better to be alone than to place your faith in another human being for fear that they would hurt and betray you as your father had done. Because it's not Mara that you're protecting. It's yourself. And knowing that you would be unable to give her the one thing she genuinely wanted, you never should have married her to begin with. But you did, because you're a selfish bastard who didn't want anyone else to have her, and then you banished her here, to this castle, where—

"Shut up," he growled.

"I—I didn't say anything, Your Grace."

"Not you, Humphrey."

"Ah—"

"Never mind." He gave an impatient jerk of his arm. "If you've never been married, then you cannot give me the advice that I seek. You are dismissed, Humphrey."

"It's true that I've yet to have the good fortune of being married, but with all due respect, Your Grace . . . neither have you."

"What's he talking about?" Ambrose grumbled under his breath after the butler had left. "I *am* married. I've been married for two damn years and have the wife to prove it."

But did he?

Did he really?

He had a wife, that much was true.

A wife he'd pushed away, ignored, and tried his best to forget. A wife who was planning to have an affair. A wife who made his blood burn like no other woman ever had.

"HUMPHREY!" he yelled again, except this time it wasn't the butler that responded, but rather another person in his life he'd taken great pains to avoid. And the sight of her face—older, more weathered, but just as kind as it had been when he was a lost, lonely little boy—shot a pang of some unidentifiable emotion straight through his cold, withered heart. "Agnes. You . . . you look well."

"I look *old*," she corrected him, wrinkles fanning out from the corners of her eyes as she smiled. "It's been a long time, Your Grace, since ye have come tae visit us here and stayed more than a night. I'm happy tae see ye."

When he was a lad, Agnes had been a young scullery maid. Nearly as far down on the servant hierarchy as one could get. Since then, she'd risen to housekeeper and, occasionally, lady's maid. The lady's maid of a duchess, and that placed her shoulder to shoulder with Humphrey, but still far, far below even the lowest titled gentry.

Ambrose and Agnes were on opposite ends of a wide, often cruel spectrum that separated those who had from those who had not. But as he stood there, gazing at the woman who had been more of a mother to him than his own, Ambrose found that nothing divided them but his own ungratefulness and detachment from anyone who meant anything.

"I apologize," he said hoarsely, causing Agnes's brow to crease.

"For what, Your Grace?"

"For . . . for . . ." But his throat thickened, making it impossible for him to get the words out. An entire decade's worth of words bottled up under layers of resentment that he'd directed at those who deserved it least. He gazed at her helplessly, silently pleading for her to understand, and, of course, she did.

Agnes always had.

"There, there," she said briskly, reaching out to give his hands a squeeze. "Nothing tae trouble yourself with. Nothing a'tall. Ye are here when ye need tae be, and I am the last tae place blame at your feet for staying away as long as ye did." Her grip tightened. "But that's not tae say there isn't someone else ye owe an explanation to."

"Mara," he said, barely suppressing a wince. Agnes might have been heartily into her sixtieth year, but the Scottish woman had the strength of an ox. "In case you hadn't heard, she wants nothing to do with me."

"And for that I *do* blame ye," Agnes said sternly. "Marrying that sweet young girl and then leaving her here at this cold, unfeeling place tae fend for herself. With all due respect, Your Grace. What in the name of the bean-nighe were ye thinking?"

"I'm starting to believe that 'with all due respect' doesn't mean what you and Humphrey think it means," he said dryly, extricating his hands from Agnes's death hold before she ground all the bones in his fingers to dust. "It is not uncommon for a husband and wife to live apart. In fact, it's *more* common than naught."

"For them, maybe," Agnes said with a dismissive turn of her wrist. "But not for ye, and certainly not for her. Ye need tae fix it."

Ambrose snorted. "A marriage isn't a torn garment to be repaired."

"Is it not? When a waistcoat is new, it's easy tae care for. A bit of cleaning now and again. But when it starts tae fray, as all clothing inevitably does, and the buttons loosen, ye have two choices. Ye can toss it away and buy another, or ye can take the time and the dedication to fix what is worn. Tae fix what ye already *know* fits ye." The housekeeper put her hands on her hips, and even though she was a good foot shorter than Ambrose's solid six feet, somehow managed to look down her nose at him. "Don't be afraid tae pick up a needle, Your Grace."

Afraid, he thought scornfully as Agnes followed in Humphrey's footsteps and quit the bedchamber. He wasn't *afraid* of his marriage or of Mara, and he'd even go so far as to prove it. But later that evening, when he went downstairs, fully expecting the Duchess of Southwick to be waiting for him in the dining room as he'd requested, she was nowhere to be seen.

"Fine," he said aloud, scowling at his soup. And then, to a

footman standing in the corner, he growled, "Take the other place setting away. The duchess will not be joining me for dinner."

If his dear, doting wife—who he was *not* afraid of—wanted to ignore a direct order and remain hidden away in her private quarters, then she could eat her supper cold. It didn't bother him one way or another. *She* didn't bother him one way or another. His earlier... reactions... were likely nothing more than a random sensitivity to dust.

Ambrose didn't love his wife.

He had to sneeze.

And that was that.

CHAPTER TEN

I F AMBROSE GENUINELY believed that she was going to join him for dinner after the way he'd treated her in the solarium, Mara fumed whilst yanking a brush through her hair, then he hadn't been paying close enough attention.

She wasn't—she refused to be—the timid, shy, weak girl that he'd abandoned here all those months ago. If she was brave enough to solicit an affair, then she could be brave enough to stand up to her brute of a husband. And that was exactly what she meant to do. Ambrose could have the privilege of dining with her when he'd *earned* it. Until then, he could do as she'd done since the last time she'd seen him.

Eat alone.

"Thank you, Agnes," she told her lady's maid after the older woman had finished fluffing her pillows and laying out a simple white nightdress adorned with lace at the scalloped neckline and sleeves. "That will be all for tonight."

"Ye have hardly touched your food," Agnes observed, frowning at the uneaten bowl of soup and bread that she'd carried up nearly an hour ago. "Ye have tae eat, Your Grace."

"I'm afraid I haven't much of an appetite tonight, but tomorrow I'll make sure to eat a hearty breakfast," Mara promised, touched—as always—by Agnes's care. Without the Scotswoman to talk to, and walk with, and while away the hours with, she surely would have been driven mad by solitude. She owed Agnes a debt larger than she could repay and would sorely miss her when she traveled to London.

Agnes clucked her tongue as she lifted the platter of food and rested it against her belly. "See that ye do. Is there anything else that ye require, Your Grace? I'd be happy tae plait your hair, if ye would like."

Mara raised a frizzled red curl and smiled wryly. "I think it's beyond plaiting at this point, but hopefully a night of sleep will flatten it back out again."

"As ye wish." But Agnes still hesitated. "Are ye sure I canna help ye with—"

"Go," she said firmly, making a shooing motion with her hand. "I don't need to be coddled or watched after. I'll be fine. I *am* fine." Thankfully, she was better at lying than she was tending to her own hair.

"But—"

"Go," she insisted. "It's getting late. Your husband is surely waiting for you."

"If you're sure there's nothing else—"

"Good*night*, Agnes."

The servant bobbed her head. "Goodnight, Your Grace. And good dreams."

Mara wasn't sure how good dreams could come of such a wretched day, but she accepted Agnes's wishes with a smile before releasing a quiet sigh of relief when the door closed. While she did want companionship, having time with her own thoughts was also a comfort. And wasn't that part of being human? To desire one thing and seek another.

Ruefully meeting her own gaze in the mirror attached to her dressing table, she gave up on taming her rebellious mane into some semblance of order and instead let the copper curls ping and spring wherever they wanted as she donned the nightdress that Agnes had put out for her.

She was in the middle of pulling it over her head, her back to the door, when she heard the quiet *click* of the latch as it swung inward on silent hinges.

"Agnes," she sighed. "I told you to go home."

But when she turned around, it wasn't Agnes standing in the doorway.

It was Ambrose.

Ambrose, tall, lean, and rakishly handsome in a shirt partially unbuttoned and a black curl dangling across his temple. Ambrose, cold, arrogant, and domineering. Ambrose, the husband she wanted to loathe . . . and was terrified to love.

Bracing an arm against the frame, he arched his brow at her. "Are you ill?"

"Ill?" she repeated, caught off guard. "No. Why would you ask that?"

"Because you were not at dinner as I told you to be. I presumed your absence must have been due to some kind of sickness and took it upon myself to check on your welfare."

She scowled at him. "I am not a *pet*, to be ordered around at your command. And since when did you start caring about my welfare? I am not sick, or ill, or otherwise indisposed. You may leave."

"I'm glad that you're not sick." Lowering his arm, he stepped fully into her bedchamber, closing the door—then locking it—behind him. "But I'm not leaving."

"Why . . ." Her tongue was stuck to the roof of her mouth. Forcibly prying it loose, she swallowed and tried again. "Why not?"

"I thought we might have another lesson." As his gaze wandered leisurely across her frame, Mara realized too late that she was standing in front of a candle . . . and the orange glow, coupled with the billowy fabric of her nightdress, enabled him to view her entire silhouette as if she were wearing nothing at all. When his eyes grew hooded and he licked his lips, she blushed and crossed her arms over her breasts.

"Ambrose—"

"*Mara*," he groaned, letting his head fall against the door with a dull *thud*. "For once, don't fight me. For once, let me in."

"Let *you* in?" she said, incredulity raising her voice an entire octave. "The doors to Southwick Castle have never been locked. You've chosen not to come here. Not to come to me. Let you in?" She put her hands on her hips. "I haven't kept you away, Ambrose. That's been entirely your own doing. And now, only when I want to go, have you finally decided to stay!"

He stared at her, a silent battle warring in the depths of his gaze. "It's more complicated than that."

"There's nothing complicated about it." Auburn tendrils snaked across her shoulders when she shook her head in frustration. "I wanted you, and you weren't here. Now I don't want you, and here you are. It's simple timing, Ambrose. You're just awful at it."

"Awful?" His brows soared as he removed his jacket. "Maybe. But if there's one thing I'm not awful at, it's *this*."

Mara wanted to say that the kiss caught her unawares, but wasn't there a part of her that had goaded him into it? That had taunted, and teased, and hoped he would storm across the room, thread his fingers through her hair, and plunder her mouth until she saw stars behind her eyelids. The swell of passion roared up and over them both; a tidal wave of lust and longing that they'd both suppressed in any manner of ways.

On their wedding night, he'd been drunk and she'd been fearful.

But tonight he was demanding . . . and she was filled with dark desire.

A slight tearing sound, a whoosh of cool air, and then Mara was naked, her inhibitions pooling at her feet along with her nightdress and what remained of her anger. She fervently returned Ambrose's kiss, her hands slipping inside his shirt to slide along his firm chest. Their tongues danced, beckoning and then retreating.

Emboldened, she nipped his top lip.

Growling, he sank his teeth into her bottom one.

Momentum carried them to the bed. She fell first, landing on her side, the blankets cold against her skin but then Ambrose was there, stretching out beside her, and he was hot, so *hot*, and his hands and mouth were everywhere. Her hair. Her neck. Her shoulders. Her breasts.

She gasped, her spine arching off the mattress, when he suckled her nipple, teasing the aroused peak with his tongue in such a way that she thought of a whirlpool swirling round and round, drawing mermaids into the depths of blissful oblivion.

Whilst his tongue teased her breasts, the fingers of one hand released the waistband of his trousers and the other toyed with the curls between her thighs. Curls that were already wet with arousal that had yet to completely fade from their earlier encounter in the solarium.

Her nails scratched his back, tracing along lines of corded muscle as her head thrashed against the pillow. When she felt his finger enter her, gliding to the first knuckle, the second, the third as her slick walls instinctively clenched around him, she tensed, anticipating a rush of old fears that never came. Instead, there was only a dewy blur of lust, like a fog sinking low over a field of wildflowers. Time sped up, slowed, and then ceased all together. What was a second, a minute, an hour when Ambrose was filling her, stretching her, driving her mad? She writhed beneath him, breaths coming in fits and pants while her heart threatened to gallop right out of her ribcage.

"Easy," he whispered, trailing his mouth along the slender curve of her neck. "Let me touch you, Mara. Let me prepare you. Another finger. That's a girl. My God." His groan vibrated against the hollow behind her ear. "Your little quim is so fucking *tight.*"

Her body was on fire. Couldn't he see that she was burning? Burning with passion, with lust, with raw, unbridled need. So much so that when he captured her wrist and guided her palm to the center of his loins where the root of his desire pulsed, she wasn't intimidated, as she'd been on their wedding night, but intrigued. Fascinated, even, by the size of him. By the smooth, silky texture. By the wet spill of seed on the pad of her thumb when she circled the throbbing tip.

He kissed her, his tongue sliding between her lips as her hand slid along his length and his fingers dipped inside her. The rhythm was . . . cataclysmic. A combination of sensation that had her bucking shamelessly against his wrist even as her own worked feverishly to deliver him the same passion that he was giving to her.

"Stop," he said hoarsely, lifting his hips away from her hand, his eyes glinting shards of demonic blue in a swarthy countenance of devilish beauty. He held her gaze as he entered her. As he slowly buried himself to the hilt.

As he set every nerve ending in her body ablaze.

On a mewling whimper of unintelligible sound, she grasped his hair, his shoulders, his back—anything tangible she could cling onto while the bed tilted and the room blurred. Was *this* what she had been missing? Was *this* what he had been keeping from her? All that time, wasted. Wandering through a desert without a drop of water. Now she was in an ocean with crashing swells, and even though it would mean drowning, she'd have joyfully thrown herself to the depths if Ambrose's arms were there to catch her.

Suddenly, without the courtesy of a warning, he began to withdraw, muscles rippling beneath her fingers, and she reflexively tightened her grip, loathe to let him go, to let this end. To put a period on a page that seemed as if it were still in mid-sentence.

"Is that it?" she asked, unable to disguise her disappointment.

His husky chuckle tickled the curls behind her ear as he skimmed his lips along her jawline. "Love, we're just beginning." Capturing her wrists, he held them above her head while he filled her again, asking—commanding—that she take every inch of him. Her back bowing, she did as he demanded, her small heels rising to hug the taut curve of his buttocks.

Their bodies began to move in unison, an ebb and flow that

was old as the tides.

New, and yet somehow familiar. Because in the end, wasn't this where they were meant to be? Wasn't this where they fit?

Where they *belonged*.

Not in different households or different towns, but here. In the same room. In the same bed. Where it was impossible to tell where she began and Ambrose ended, caught in a friction of intimacy that far surpassed the physical.

Candlelight, gold and flickering, danced across skin damp with desire. Their blood hummed, a distant roar of a waterfall pounding on the rock below. Their breathing quickened; his harsh and deep, hers quick and shallow. Racing, yearning, *reaching* for what was promised but unspoken. For what was wanted but unknown.

Putting his hand between them, Ambrose found the source of all her pleasure. A single stroke as he plunged his hips forward and Mara . . . Mara was lost.

IN THE AFTERMATH, in the quiet reverberations that came after a rolling storm when the winds had eased and the rain had stopped, Mara lay tucked up against her husband's side with his arm draped across her waist. By the slow rise and fall of his chest, she could tell that if sleep hadn't claimed him yet, it would very soon. As for her, she was wide awake. Her eyes open. Her limbs pleasantly heavy. Her cheeks aching from the duration of her smile.

After being a virgin bride for so long, she was finally, *finally* a wife. And while she hated the road that had brought her here, she wouldn't have changed the destination.

"Ambrose?" she whispered, tilting her chin to her shoulder in an attempt to see if he was still with her. "Are you awake?"

"Barely," came the muffled response, and her smile widened.

"That was . . . what we did . . . well, I don't have the right words." Truth be told, she didn't know if there *were* words to describe what had happened in this bed. "But . . . I liked it. Very much. I just . . . I wanted to tell you that."

A long pause.

Too long.

It was *too long*, and her smile had already started to falter at the edges even before he said, "I'm glad you enjoyed your second lesson."

The slash of a whip on exposed skin would have stung less, but she reacted the same. Flinching, she rolled away from him and sat up on her side, drawing the blanket to her breasts. "Don't say that, Ambrose. Don't call it *that*."

If he hadn't been fully awake before, he was now. Putting his arms behind his head, he regarded her with a cool, distant expression that made her want to alternately shake him and pull her own hair.

"Have your plans changed, then?" he asked. "Do you still intend to go to London and take a lover?"

If she were sitting beside the Ambrose of five minutes ago, she would have said no in a heartbeat. In *less* than a heartbeat. But this Ambrose wasn't that Ambrose. This was an entirely different man. A different husband. A stranger in her bed.

How she despised how quickly he was capable of changing from one to the other! Shedding his emotions like a coat. Donning whatever clothing suited him. Whatever clothing protected him. Because that's what he was doing. That's what they were *both* doing, she acknowledged dimly. Protecting themselves. Like wounded wolves reaching out to nuzzle the hand that fed it one second . . . and drawing blood the next. Incapable of trusting that this time, this time, this *one* precious time that could change everything if they allowed it, the person they wanted desperately to love wasn't going to lead them into despair.

He was hurting her before she hurt him. Defending himself

before she'd even landed a blow.

And maybe if she weren't equally afraid, she might have been able to push past his defenses. To lay herself bare. To make herself vulnerable. To let hope in at the risk of her own harm. But she wasn't strong enough. She wasn't brave enough. After years of being pushed down, of being quiet, of learning that the best way to avoid pain was to hide, she lacked the ability to stand.

"That depends," she said carefully. It was the best that she could manage, the most that she could give, and as a reward, she watched his gaze shutter and felt her stomach sink.

"Then I'll call it a lesson because that's what it was."

"Where are you going?" she said when he climbed out of bed and strode, naked, to the blue room door.

"To get some bloody sleep."

"Ambrose—"

"What?" he snarled, brows snapping together over the bridge of his nose.

"Nothing," she said softly. "Nothing at all."

⟫⟫⟩⟨⟨⟨

FOR THE SECOND night in a row, Ambrose waited impatiently for Mara to appear for dinner. Aside from a brief and accidental crossing of paths in the garden, they'd not spoken since the night before when his dust sensitivity had flared and he'd experienced the most earth-shattering orgasm of his entire bloody life . . . followed by a quagmire of emotion that he'd had no idea what to do with.

That depends, she'd said when he asked her if she planned to seek companionship outside the bounds of their marriage. Two tiny words that had brought on such a surge of anger, of unadulterated rage, that if he'd not walked out when he had, he was almost certain he would have left something broken in his wake.

JILLIAN EATON

Not Mara.

He'd never lay a finger on Mara.

Never hurt a beautiful red hair on her infuriatingly stubborn little head.

But that ugly vase in the corner that he'd never particularly cared for . . . well, suffice it to say, that vase wouldn't have stood a chance.

The worst of it was that he had not gone into her room with the intention of bedding her.

Very well, the thought had crossed his mind.

Briefly.

A dozen times.

In a single hour.

But that wasn't why he'd paid her a visit. He'd wanted to tell her how cross he was with her for ignoring his request to join him for dinner. He'd wanted to communicate his annoyance. Wasn't that what married couples did? They *communicated*. But then she'd looked at him. A single look with those big doe eyes still sparkling with indignation from his earlier behavior (which had been, admittedly, quite boorish), and he was lost.

Lost to reason.

Lost to feeling.

Lost to Mara.

But that was then, and this was now, and where the hell was she? He'd sent a note, hadn't he? A polite note requesting her presence in the dining room at precisely half past six. Except the last he'd checked, it was a quarter beyond seven . . . and it was clear that she intended to defy him again.

Cutting forcefully into the main course—roasted boar stuffed with apples and bathed in a blackberry-honey mustard sauce—he was in the middle of slaughtering the poor pig for a second time when an eerie, violent howl echoed through the house. Freezing mid-slice, Ambrose frowned at the footman standing in the corner. "What the devil was that noise?"

"There's been a pack of wild dogs attacking livestock

throughout the village," said the servant, his face paling. "We've managed to keep them away from the castle by rounding up our animals at night and housing them in the barns, but by the sound of it, something's lured them close to the house."

Something . . .

Or someone.

Mara.

From their courtship, he knew that his wife had a habit of walking when she was troubled . . . and last night they hadn't exactly parted on the best of terms.

Grabbing the knife he'd just been using to cut his roast into mincemeat, Ambrose bolted from the dining room.

CHAPTER ELEVEN

THAT EVENING, NOT ready to face Ambrose again so soon, Mara chose to skip dinner once again and go for a walk instead. The wind ruffled her hair as she followed a lesser traveled path around the outskirts of the orchards, the cool wind undercut with a sweet breeze that hinted at warmer weather soon to come.

Already most of the trees were beginning to grow shy green buds. Before those buds grew into leaves, she would be on her way to London, having placated Kitty enough that her sister's offer of room and board remained available to her . . . in spite of whatever issues had arisen between Kitty and William. Issues that Kitty had refused to elaborate on, other than to say the decision to divorce had been made, and she cared not to discuss the matter any further.

They'd been through a lot, she and her sister.

More than two defenseless girls should ever have to endure.

But Mara wasn't about to allow the shadows of her past—or the surly duke in her present—ruin her future. Her father and her husband be damned, she was finally going to do what *she* wanted to do. And she wouldn't feel guilty about it or jump through obstacles like some trained circus pony. Short of physically binding her to Southwick Castle, what could Ambrose do to keep her here?

Make love to me in the light of the moon and then crush my heart to dust in the darkness.

"Nothing," she said with a fierceness that had the unfortunate habit of only making itself known when he wasn't around. "Absolutely nothing."

Once, not so very long ago by the standards of time (and yet so long ago by the standards of emotion that it almost felt like a different lifetime), she and Ambrose had walked through an orchard together. Peaches, she recalled. A rare treat that required dedication and determination to grow, as the fruit wasn't native to England's colder summer and rockier soil. History books on horticulture credited Alexander the Great with bringing the first peach tree to England after conquering Persia, and from there it had become a symbol of wealth to have a peach tree flowering in one's garden.

The orchard that she and Ambrose had visited during another courtship outing was part of Kensington Gardens, a place of great beauty and prestige that had been denied to her when she was the daughter of a viscount with no political or social affiliation of note, but opened for a private tour without question when she arrived the Duke of Southwick's arm.

"What are you doing?" Ambrose had asked her, his mouth quirking in bemusement when she'd stopped just inside the gate and extended her fingertips out to the side, her entire body trembling at the sheer joy of being surrounded by such opulent greenery.

"Trying to decide," she'd replied.

"Decide what?"

"On where to go first."

"That's easy," he'd murmured, draping his arm around her waist and giving her an entirely different reason to tremble. Their chaperone for the day was an elderly second cousin with diminished vision who had already settled herself onto a nearby bench to take a nap in the shade . . . leaving the duke's hands free to wander where they willed. "We can go wherever we like. The grounds, Lady Marabelle, are yours, for as long as you'd like them."

Some men charmed the objects of their affection with jewelry.

Others with trinkets, or furs, or even horses.

But Ambrose . . . Ambrose had given her Kensington Gardens. Of all the places available to him in London, he'd brought her *here*. And maybe it was an absent gesture. An idea plucked from obscurity. But she liked to believe—she wanted to believe—that it meant something. That he was beginning to know her, as she'd always hoped that a man one day would. The quiet, hidden parts of her that no one else seemed to care about. Her interests and her hobbies. What made her smile. What lifted her heart. What brought her joy.

"Why don't we start at the native ferns?" she said, her smile hardly able to fit her face. "Then make our way toward the climbing roses. I read in *Mansfield's Flora and Fauna Daily* a new variety was recently grafted that is specifically resistant to the red spider mite!"

"How fascinating," Ambrose said dryly, and Mara blushed as she realized how she must have sounded.

"I'm sorry. I . . . I have an unnatural affinity for plants. I didn't mean to bore you."

"Bore me?" Blue eyes captured hers as he stepped in front of her and lifted her chin on the crook of his gloved knuckle. "You could recite the alphabet a thousand times over and never bore me, Lady Marabelle."

Her blush deepened; a warm pink wave spreading from her cheeks to her chest. "You're merely saying that to humor me."

The duke's mouth twisted in an amused smirk. "I am a remarkably busy man. I haven't the time or the inclination to say things that I don't mean."

A busy man who had devoted his entire day to her.

How wonderfully foreign, the notion that she was worthy of being made a priority.

"Thank you," she said softly, glancing to the side. She found it difficult to look at the duke for any great length of time. He was too bright. Too powerful. And the ideas that those sharp cheekbones and wicked lips put inside her head were much too impure for a virgin wallflower to entertain.

"For what?" Ambrose asked, lifting a dark brow.

"For making me feel . . . special."

The hand on her chin went to her cheek, then to her hair, fingers gliding through the curls peeking out from beneath the straw bonnet she wore. "You are special," he said, his voice husky in a way that made her knees go weak. "I won't hear you speak otherwise."

The butterflies dancing on the flowers and the butterflies in Mara's belly exploded into colorful flight as he followed the curve of her ear with his thumb, lightly massaging the sensitive lobe where she wore simple pearl earrings that had once belonged to her mother. He lowered his head as if to whisper a secret, and her nipples tingled when he replaced his thumb with his teeth, delivering an impish bite that he immediately soothed with his tongue. Before meeting the duke, she'd never known how provocative an ear could be . . . or that there was a line of connection between her hearing and her breasts.

"Your Grace," she protested weakly, willing her hand between them to push against his chest with nominal force. Were he a feather, she wouldn't have knocked him over. But then, she didn't want to. Not really. She merely wanted to *look* like she did. "We—we shouldn't. Not in public."

His lips grazed the length of her neck. "I don't see the ferns complaining."

Mara suddenly had a sneaking suspicion that Ambrose's desire to tour Kensington Gardens had little to do with her love for plants and much more to do with being in a place that assured solitude. Aside from their chaperone, who was already snoring, and a stonemason working on a retaining wall beside one of the ponds, they were completely alone. Something they hadn't been since after the theater when he'd kissed her in the rain.

"Do you know that they have a peach orchard here?" she asked breathlessly.

With a mild grunt of irritation, the duke raised his head. "Is that really what you want to do? Admire peaches?" His eyebrows waggled. "Because I can think of another peach I'd like to admire that doesn't grow on a tree."

"Your *Grace*," she gasped when he reached around and pinched her bottom.

"I'm sorry," he said gravely, linking his arms behind his back. "I've overstepped the bounds of propriety. Do accept my apology."

Her eyes narrowed. "You're not sorry at all, are you?"

"Not even the smallest bit," he replied with a roguish grin.

Even though she shouldn't have, Mara liked this side of himself that the Duke of Southwick was sharing with her. She'd already discerned, during their limited outings together, that he had several.

Most often he was aloof and reserved. Other times he was quick with a barb that stung just a little too sharply. But when he relaxed and let his guard fall enough to let a genuine smile slip through the cynical set of his lips . . . that was the Ambrose she loved the best.

Liked, she corrected herself hastily.

That was the side of Ambrose that she *liked* the best.

And now who was hiding parts of themselves?

"The . . . the orchard is that way, I believe," she said, pointing to the right.

He gestured to the path in front of them. "Then lead the way, my lady."

Over the next four hours, Mara and Ambrose explored nearly every inch of riches that the gardens had to offer. They studied the various types of ferns. They found the climbing roses. They even shared a freshly ripened peach, and Mara blushed all over again when the duke licked the juice from her fingers.

"Delicious," he said after releasing her pinky with an audible *pop* of suction that made the muscles in her belly quiver. "I'll make sure my gardener puts in an orchard at Southwick Castle."

"That is your country estate?" she queried as they began a wandering journey back toward the front gates where their chaperone was, presumably, still snoring away.

"Yes, it is." He toyed with a loose tendril at the nape of her neck. "There are apples and pears. Even a grove of orange trees in the conservatory. But to the best of my knowledge, no peaches."

A real conservatory.

How marvelous!

The closest thing she had to an indoor greenhouse was a weed growing in the sill of her bedroom window.

"Do you travel to Southwick Castle often? It sounds beautiful."

A shadow crossed his countenance. "No."

No, he didn't go there, or no, it wasn't beautiful? Mara wanted him to elaborate, but it was clear by the pulse of a muscle high in his jaw that the estate was a topic he did not care to discuss, similar to his parents. When she'd asked him about them before, he'd bristled like a bear. A bear with very sharp, very dangerous teeth. Not wanting to feel the chomp of a bite, she'd let the matter drop. But how was she supposed to know if they were compatible enough for marriage if she didn't know him?

"Your Grace," she began, raising her skirts as they stepped onto a small bridge. "What do you—"

"Lilacs," he interrupted.

Mara frowned. "Pardon?"

"Every person has an individual scent." He stopped in the middle of the bridge and suddenly she found herself pressed against the railing, his arms trapping her on either side as his mouth hovered in the space where passion and possibility collided. "Yours is a bloom of lilacs on the first day of spring. When the ground is still frozen, and the air is sharp, but the lilacs . . ." Lowering his head, he nuzzled her neck. "The lilacs are sweet."

Who knew, she thought dazedly, that the Duke of Southwick was such a poet? A poet *and* a pianist, his lips flitting across her flushed skin like fingers on keys. He played her expertly, drawing forth notes and chords that she hadn't even realized were trapped inside of her. Notes and chords that created a beautiful, haunting melody of wanting and desire.

Whilst the birds sang, and the brook babbled, and the roses bloomed, Ambrose kissed her with an almost lazy intensity, as if they were on the first movement of a classical symphony with three more to go. His tongue languished in her mouth, stroking and then retreating, thrusting and then parrying, before he sank his teeth into her bottom lip, eliciting a moan of pure pleasure.

It was a fanciful imagining, but Mara couldn't help but wonder if this was how a flower felt when it yielded its nectar to a bee. Drinking up the sun one moment, surrendering itself to a fierce adversary the next. Except the bee wasn't *truly* an adversary, because along with the nectar, it was also taking pollen, that magical yellow dust that allowed flowers to spread, and grow, and thrive.

Was that what Ambrose was doing for her?

Doing *to* her?

Clasping her hips, he turned her around so that she was overlooking the water while he kissed the side of her throat and his hands teased their way up her waist to cup her breasts, touching her where she'd touched herself in the dim and the darkness.

"Do you like that?" he whispered—the voice of the devil purring in her ear—and she nodded helplessly, her head lolling onto his shoulder as the music built. Taking her arm by the wrist, he drew it down, down, down to the v-shaped garden below her hips where he took precious care to align her fingers over the damp curls hidden beneath layers of thin cotton and muslin. "Are you slick with wanting, Lady Marabelle? Are you pulsing with it?"

A shy pause, a galloping heart, and then she nodded again . . . transforming from a pianoforte to a flower, then to a marionette as he guided her hand, using it as if it were an object solely designed for his pleasure instead of an appendage of her own body.

Using it as if it belonged to him.

As if *she* belonged to him.

And heaven help her immortal soul, but in that moment . . . in that moment, she wanted to. In that moment, she would have given anything—she would have given *everything*—to be his.

Manipulated by her own fingers (which, in the duke's grasp, were far more deft at delivering sexual gratification than when she was in sole control of them), Mara began to rock her hips back and forth, unconsciously rubbing the curve of her bottom along the rigid shaft contained within Ambrose's trousers.

Groaning into her hair, he centered her in the middle of his body and continued to guide her wrist in increasingly rapid undulations so that she was pleasuring herself in the front and him behind, all while the day continued on around them with gardeners gardening and chaperones sleeping and the busy world beyond completely oblivious to what passions were occurring on an unassuming little wooden bridge in the middle of Kensington Gardens between a mighty duke and a wide-eyed wallflower.

When the crescendo began to build for the fourth movement, Mara stiffened, her willowy frame going taut as a violin string. On a gasping cry that a bird enthusiast on the far end of the park confused for the call of a brown thrasher, she came at her own hand. A breath later and the duke followed suit, yanking her tight against him while he thrusted his loins forward, pinning her to the railing. She clutched the wood, bending over it as the symphony reached its final climax. There was a desperate rising swell of music, a song caught on the trembling edge of a heartbeat, and then absolute silence . . . silence save for the duke's ragged exhale in her ear.

He released his grasp on her arm, leaving a wrinkled glove in his wake. A glove that she would go on later that night to fold carefully away in the cedar trunk under her bed, where she kept her most precious belongings, never to be worn again.

She turned around just as he was running a hand across his face, leaving his expression temporarily unguarded. In his gaze she saw a flicker of disbelief, almost awe, and below that . . . below that was such an earnest *yearning* that she found herself battling back a rush of tears.

Mara knew what it was like to want something. To want something with a fierceness that consumed all that you were.

For her, it was freedom. Freedom from her tyrant of a father. Freedom from the nightmares of her past. Freedom to become more than she was born to be.

And while she had no idea what a *duke* could want that he didn't already have, like recognized like. Pain recognized pain. Hurt recognized hurt.

Reaching for his hand, she gently linked their fingers and his countenance immediately shuttered.

"Lady Marabelle, I must apologize—"

"I'll do it," she said, her eyes wide with a mixture of uncertainty and hope.

"You'll do what?" he said warily.

"I'll marry you. That is why you've been courting me, isn't it?" When the uncertainty began to overshadow the hope, she snatched her hand away and wondered if the water under the bridge was deep enough to drown herself in. "I . . . I'm sorry. Never mind. I was being terribly presumptuous, and I . . . I . . . I don't know what I'm doing," she whispered haltingly.

The corners of Ambrose's lips gave the tiniest of twitches. "That much is obvious. But you're right. I *have* been courting you with the intention of proposing. You merely beat me to it, and we can't have that, can we?"

Mutely, Mara shook her head.

"Good. Then we're in agreement." He tucked a loose curl behind her ear, the pad of his thumb lingering on the delicate shell before he let his arm fall. "But it won't be now, and it won't be here, and it won't be in these clothes."

She glanced down. "What's wrong with my clothes?"

A wry grin overtook the duke's mouth as he buttoned his burgundy tailcoat, shifting the rectangular flaps inward to cover the front panel of his trousers. "It's not *your* clothes I'm worried about. Shall we see if we can summon Cousin Beatrice from her coma?"

Now it was Mara's lips that twitched. "We likely should, lest she become a permanent fixture in the gardens. And then who would chaperone us?"

"Who indeed?" he asked, a devilish glint in his eye.

Together, they went to rouse Cousin Beatrice from her slumber.

LOST IN HER thoughts of the past, Mara did not pay close attention to where she was walking in the present. Why would she? She had traversed these paths hundreds—no, thousands—of times before.

By herself.

Almost always by herself.

With only her shadow, long and flickering, to keep her company.

There was no shadow tonight. Not with clouds keeping the half-moon under a cloak of darkness. On a shiver, Mara grasped her own cloak and gathered the folds tightly beneath her chin . . . right before she heard a low, menacing growl coming from a thicket of bramble at the edge of the orchard.

Her first instinct was to run. A child's instinct, born of learning that if she could run and hide somewhere her father's hands couldn't reach, then she'd be safe.

But there were no broom closets out here.

No tables.

No beds.

There was just Mara, the apple trees, and whatever lurked in the thorns.

"Go a-away," she said loudly, or as loudly as she could with fear wrapping itself around her vocal cords like spindly vines. When she snuck a glance over her shoulder, she realized just how far she'd let herself wander from the main house. The castle was a mere shimmer of faded gold candlelight in a swath of inky obsidian.

She was too far to run.

Too far to yell.

Too far for anyone to save her.

She was completely alone, as she'd so often been.

Another growl, longer and louder than the first. Mara wondered, almost hysterically, if Ambrose would care if she died.

Would he mourn her passing? Or would he be grateful?

Would her death be a burden? Or a relief?

When the vines began to tighten and choke, she fought against them, willing herself to remain calm. Help may not have been arriving on a white steed, but she wasn't a helpless damsel incapable of rescuing herself.

She was strong, and she was smart, and she had not survived a poor, violent childhood to die a duchess on the grounds of an estate.

"Go away," she repeated, and this time she did not stutter. Spying a branch on the ground leftover from pruning, she snatched it up and held it as a knight would a sword, swinging it from side to side. Maybe they'd find her body in pieces, but beside the pieces would be this stick, and at least they'd know she had defended herself.

The growls intensified and grew in number, some high-pitched, others low and guttural, filling her head with images of sharp fangs and glinting red eyes and bristling fur.

Wielding her branch, she spun in a circle, slicing at shadows that weren't shadows, at dogs that weren't dogs. The creatures that snapped and snarled from the bushes were closer to wolves of old than the darling spaniels and loyal terriers that had crossed to create them. Freedom had turned the pack feral and then starvation had made it wild, taking what once was tame and twisting it into something else entirely.

Something that had her surrounded.

Gathering the courage she'd lacked in the bedroom—that she'd lacked for her entire life—Mara prepared to fight.

CHAPTER TWELVE

W HERE THE HELL *was she*, Ambrose thought irritably for the second time that night as he stalked across the lawn, arms swinging at his sides. A small army of servants, organized by Humphrey, were fanning out across the rest of the grounds. Some to the stables. Some to the pond. Some to the gardens. Not wanting to wait, Ambrose had struck out on his own. As he walked, he noted a chill in the air that should haven't been there. A prickle at his nape where his hair stood on end. Was it a warning of ominous happenings on the horizon? Or merely nature's harbinger of a late frost? Either way, he would have vastly preferred to be in his study, a warm drink in his hand, instead of marching out into the darkness clutching a knife.

He didn't want to stab a dog.

He wasn't a monster.

And he *wasn't* his father.

But then an eerie howl, vicious and victorious, made his blood run cold, and he lifted his arm, pointing his weapon straight and true as he charged toward the apple orchards at the top of the hill.

"MARA!" he bellowed, his chest burning with fire and fear as he reached the first row of trees, their spindly, gnarled limbs creating a wooden labyrinth that was nearly impossible to see through. "MARA, WHERE ARE YOU?"

A chorus of barks, somewhere off to his right. He spun blindly toward the sound. The clouds parted, allowing a sliver of moonlight to slip through and reflect off the flat of his blade as a shadow leapt and his wrist sliced instinctively through the air.

The dog yelped when the point of the knife pierced its skin and deflected off a rib. Tail tucked, teeth bared, it scuttled to the side where it was joined by another pack-mate that glared at Ambrose with a flat, chilling yellow gaze.

"What the *fuck* have you done to my wife?" he snarled, more animal than man as he advanced on the wild dogs, driving them farther back into the orchard even as more crept around to flank him from behind. The bastards had him encircled, but it wasn't himself he was afraid for. It was Mara.

Mara, who had gone walking after dark because of him and his bloody callousness. Mara, who had never been anything but sweet, honest, and true. Mara, who hadn't deserved to be abandoned here as if she were something that he was ashamed of instead of the best thing that had ever happened to him.

If she died . . .

If she was already dead . . .

No.

No.

"MARA!" This time there was an undercurrent of desperation in his voice. Of despair. Of the same desolation he'd felt whenever his father had purposefully ripped his most beloved people and pets away from him in an effort to make him stronger . . . when, in the end, all it had done was turn him to stone.

Mara, for as long as they'd been apart, was and always had been the final chink in his armor. The last piece of his mortality. Just *knowing* she was here, at Southwick Castle, had been a comfort to him. A soothing balm to his tortured soul, whether he'd realized it or not. If he lost her, then he'd be reduced to nothing more than a gruesome shadow of his former self. A walking gargoyle that truly had no reason to care for anyone or anything.

She was the part of his heart that still beat.

She was the part of his soul that still felt.

She was the best of him.

She always had been.

And perhaps . . . perhaps that was why he'd been drawn to her from the very first night he'd seen her, sitting there in a ballroom with an open book on her lap. Blissfully oblivious to the catty politics and social games being played all around her. He had told himself he picked her because she was obedient and quiet: the perfect duchess for a duke who didn't want the obligations of a wife. But these past few days in her company had uncovered a difficult truth.

He could have picked anyone.

But he'd *chosen* Mara.

Not for her submissiveness or her obedience, but because from their first words spoken, to their first kiss, to the first time she'd made him laugh, she had made him feel whole again. She had made him feel like he had a home again. A real home, the kind that he'd yearned for all those years when he was a sad little boy who had just wanted his parents to love him as he was.

Mara had been willing to love him as he was. She'd accepted his numerous flaws. She'd softened his hardest edges. She'd made him better.

And in return, he'd ignored her. He'd pushed her away. He'd banished her. Because the need to prove that he wasn't worth loving was far stronger and more ingrained than the vulnerability it took to be lovable.

"Ambrose?" Mara's call was weak and came from the middle of the orchards, but the sound of it—the sweet, sweet angelic sound—made him stop in his tracks and sent his frozen blood pumping anew.

With purpose.

With power.

With protectiveness.

Mara was *his* wife, dammit. She belonged to *him*. And no one—not some prancing dandy or a pack of feral hounds—was going to take her. To hell with lists of eligible bachelors. To hell with lessons in seduction. And to hell with these *fucking* dogs.

Attacking with brute savagery, he flung them out of his way left and right, plowing ahead toward the sound of Mara's cry as they snapped at his heels and tore at his clothing. Sharp teeth sank into his calf, a brilliant, burning pain that he barely acknowledged before he kicked the dog off and kept running.

Thin branches whipped at his face and chest as he charged through the long rows of apple trees. His heart pounding, his breath coming in ragged fits and starts, he ran to Mara as if he were a knight charging up the hill of battle to save the princess from the dragon at the gates . . . except when he finally found her, she was doing a damned good job at saving herself.

"Get back!" she yelled at the three dogs that had her cornered. Wielding a long, pointy stick that whistled as it swung through the air, she struck one of the mutts in the head and caught the front legs of another. "I said *get back!*"

The branch clipped the muzzle of the third dog. The leader, if its sheer size was any indication. Hackles raised and lips peeled back, it stood its ground for the longest second of Ambrose's life . . . and then, without another sound, turned tail and slunk away into the underbrush. After a moment's hesitation—as if they were stunned their alpha had been bested by a tiny slip of a woman with nothing more than a broken off branch to defend herself with—the rest of the pack followed.

"*Mara.*" Dropping his knife, Ambrose closed the distance between them in a single stride. He gripped her shoulders, his fingers tightening around her cloak when he saw the whites of her eyes. "Mara, it's all right. They've gone. You're safe."

"Safe," she repeated in a daze, her gaze unfocused and her body trembling.

"Yes. Yes, you're safe. I've got you." He pulled her against him, pulled her *into* him, his arms wrapping her up as if she were the most precious gift on earth, and she was, that's exactly what she was, and why the hell had it taken her almost being snatched away from him to realize it? "I'm sorry, Mara." Dimly, he was aware of a growing numbness in his leg. A tingling that was spreading with pointy little pins from his calf to his knee to his thigh. "I'm sorry I wasn't here when you needed me."

"Ambrose?" As the shock began to fade and the fog cleared from her eyes, Mara blinked up at him in astonishment. "Ambrose . . . you . . . you came for me?"

"Always," he returned gruffly. "From this day forth, I'll always come for you. Mara, I . . ."

Her lips parted when he trailed off. "You what, Ambrose?"

"I . . ." Abruptly releasing his hold on her, he staggered sideways as the trees spun around him in a dizzying circle. "I . . . I don't feel well."

And with that, the mighty Duke of Southwick collapsed to the ground in a dead faint.

≫≫≪≪

IT TOOK FOUR men, and Mara cradling Ambrose's head, to carry him all the way back to the castle and up to his private chamber.

"I'll fetch the doctor," said Agnes after taking one look at the duke's ashen countenance. "He lives on the other side of the village and can be here within the hour. We'll send our fastest horse and footman." Patting Mara's arm, she tried to gently coax her away from the bed. "Ye have had quite the ordeal yourself, my dear. Let's get ye out of those clothes and a warm broth in your belly. Maybe even a hot bath."

"No," Mara said with a vehement shake of her head. "I won't leave him. Not when I don't even know what's wrong!" Clutching Ambrose's hand, she willed him to wake up. To open his eyes. To yell at her. To do anything but just lay there, as still and silent as a corpse. "He was fine. He was—he was about to tell me something. Something important. And then..." Tears threatened and she battled them back, willing herself to be as strong inside the house as she'd been outside of it. "Please," she whispered, not taking her gaze off Ambrose's face. "Please tell the footman to hurry."

Agnes glanced at Humphrey, who had been charged with getting the duke from the orchards to his chambers. The butler's expression of muted concern mirrored her own. It was frightful to see His Grace in such a state of debilitating weakness. He was well and thoroughly unconscious, with nary a movement of his little finger to be seen. He was also pale, and—in Agnes's opinion, who wasn't a doctor, but had tended plenty a scratch and cut amidst the maids—growing paler by the second. Never a good sign. But he was also a hale, hearty man in the prime of his life. What could have cut him down with the quickness of an axe felling an oak tree?

"The dogs," she said suddenly, and both Humphrey and Mara swung their heads to look at her. She'd already ordered everyone else from the room. "Ye said ye weren't bit, Your Grace, but was the duke?"

Mara looked at her husband.

Always.

From this day forth, I'll always come for you.

I...

I...

How she wished he'd finished that sentence! Possibly the most important sentence of their entire marriage. He had to be all right. He just had to be. Because as difficult as it was to love Ambrose, it would be even harder to lose him.

"I'm not sure." She squeezed his hand. "If he was, he didn't mention it. But it all happened so fast. Do you think a bite would have done this?"

"Not a single bite. Not on its own. Although..."

"What? What is it?"

"We need tae remove his clothing. Every stitch. And I'll need a bucket of hot water. Steaming. Along with clean linens. An entire stack of them. Well, Mr. Humphrey? What are ye still doing there? Go!" Agnes said, shooing the butler from the room. "Go, go! And close the door behind ye."

"Remove his clothing?" Mara said, bewildered. "Why would we do that?"

"Because if he was bitten, and lost enough blood as a result, then this is what he'd look like." Agnes went around to the other side of the bed and began to unbutton Ambrose's waistcoat, her fingers moving quickly and efficiently down the row of buttons. "I've seen an ashen complexion like this before, in a mother that kept bleeding after the babe was born. There's no time tae lose. We have tae find the source of the blood loss and stop it."

Mara went to the foot of the bed and took off Ambrose's boots. "What happened? To the mother."

Agnes stopped mid-button. "She died."

Mara gasped. "Ambrose—"

"His Grace is fit," Agnes cut in. "He is young, and hale, and hearty. He'll be back tae yelling at all of us before we know it, and then we'll *wish* he was in the state that he is now."

Despite the terror coursing through her veins, the older Scottish woman's words managed to coax forth the slightest smile. "He doesn't yell as much as he broods. And grumbles. And glares."

"Aye," Agnes agreed, finishing with the waistcoat and moving onto the linen shirt beneath it. Proceeding with care, she lifted the duke's arms one at a time to slide them free of the long sleeves, baring his muscular chest to the orange glow of candlelight. "He was always fond of a good glare, even as a lad. But I canna blame him, as his father was ten times worse and quick with a fist besides."

"He was beaten?" Mara said softly, her heart giving a painful lurch inside her chest. She would never be able to understand how a parent, whose singular duty was to protect their child, could be capable of harming them. Why even *have* children if your intention was to hurt? To frighten? To scar? Had the late duke's father hit him, and that was why he'd hit Ambrose? She'd often wondered if that was the case with her own father. Once the initial lash of pain had faded, she had wanted a reason. And even though an explanation wouldn't have solved the matter or stopped it from happening again, at least it would have given her someone to blame other than herself.

"I spoke out of turn, Your Grace. Forgive me." Folding Ambrose's shirt into a neat square, Agnes set it aside and took a breath. "I don't see any wounds or abrasions. We'll have tae remove his boots and trousers. If you'd rather me call for a maid—"

"He's my husband," Mara interrupted. "If anyone is going to remove his clothes, it should be me." But her hands still trembled as she carefully loosened the gusset ties on either side of his waist.

Working together, she and Agnes managed to roll him to the left and then to the right, one of them propping his hip up while the other pulled his boots off one at a time. What they uncovered made Mara gasp aloud.

"Oh, Ambrose," she cried, instinctively recoiling from the torn flesh underneath his right knee. Flesh torn by a wild dog with sharp, ripping teeth. Pressure from his boot must have acted like a tourniquet and temporarily slowed the flow of blood emptying into it, but with it removed the wound bled like a river, staining the blankets and the mattress an awful, awful red. "I don't—I don't know what to do." Her hands fluttered helplessly. "Agnes, what do we *do?*"

Mara had grown up learning how to heal tiny cuts and hide small bruises. But this wound, this terrible, life-threatening wound, was far beyond her capabilities.

The dread that filled her, like a syrup that was too sweet and sticky, made the fear she'd experienced in the orchards pale in comparison. At least amidst the trees, she'd been able to defend herself. To fight back. But here, in her husband's private chambers, with him lying on his bed still as death itself while his blood dripped steadily onto the floor with a sickly *plop, plop, plop,* she couldn't think of a single thing within her power that would aid him.

She wasn't a doctor or a midwife.

Before last night, she hadn't even been a wife.

But she wanted to be. Oh, how she wanted to be.

Don't die, she thought silently, grabbing his hand and gazing intently at his face because she couldn't stand to look at what was below his knee. *Please don't die. I don't know how to save you. I don't know how to save us. But I do know that there is something here worth saving. Underneath all of the harsh words, and the bitter mistakes, and the unbearable loneliness . . . there's something that can still grow. I'm sure of it.*

Where her conviction came from, she hadn't a clue. But she felt it inside of her, as surely as she felt the frantic beat of her heart.

"Ye keep holding onto him, Your Grace," Agnes said, nodding at Mara's sure grip around Ambrose's fingers. "That's all ye have tae do. Mr. Humphrey and I will take care of the rest, and the doctor when he arrives."

"I can do that," Mara murmured, sinking into a crouch beside the bed. "I've already held on for nearly two years. I can hold on for as long as it takes."

When the butler rushed in with all of the supplies Agnes had ordered, she held on. When the doctor came and said they had to cauterize the wound to stop the bleeding, she held on. When the hot iron sizzled against her husband's flesh, she held on. When they wrapped the leg in white bandages and said there was nothing else to be done but wait, she held on. And when sleep finally claimed her, she laid her head against the edge of the mattress . . . and she held on.

CHAPTER THIRTEEN

May 1811
St Mary Abbots Church
London, England

"KITTY, I'M NERVOUS," said Mara, fidgeting in place as she stood in front of a double set of towering wooden doors. In a moment—in mere seconds—those doors would open, the music would start, and she would march forward to her new husband. Her new life. Her new beginning. She was a caterpillar completing its final transformation into a butterfly, its wings struggling to squeeze through the tiny opening at the top of the chrysalis.

But what if she *wanted* to be a caterpillar?

"Nervous?" Kitty, beautiful as always in a pink gown and matching crown of flowers, rolled her eyes. "What's there to be nervous about? You're about to be a duchess."

"There are two hundred people in there." Reaching under the voluminous folds of her dress, an ivory concoction of layered muslin and scalloped lace, Mara scratched her ankle, then her calf, then her knee. She was so *itchy*.

"All waiting to see you. And me." Kitty flashed a brilliant smile that faded as she begrudgingly added, "But mostly you."

"I told Ambrose I wanted a small affair," she muttered, dropping her skirt. "He said his mother wouldn't hear of it. I'm scared of her. The duchess. She's so . . . cold."

"The *dowager* duchess, you mean," Kitty corrected as she knelt behind Mara and fussed with her very long, very impractical train. "And it's better that she's too cold than too warm. William's mother is constantly asking me to tea, and to go shopping, and to attend charity functions with her. The woman is *exhausting.*"

Two weeks ago, Kitty had begun courting William Colborne, Earl of Radcliffe. As the grandson of a duke, he was second in line for the title that Kitty truly coveted. But, as she'd told Mara, he was a most excellent kisser.

"I'd like it if Ambrose's mother wanted to go shopping." Mara clasped her hands together and resisted the urge to peel off her gloves and scratch between her fingers. "Instead she just . . . frowns at me."

Kitty straightened. "Didn't you say that she spends most of her time at an estate in the country?"

"Yes, she's only in London for the wedding."

"Well, there you have it. Problem solved."

But as the doors abruptly swung inward and the organist began to play, Mara had the distinctly uneasy feeling that her problems were just beginning.

>>>«««

"THAT WENT MORE quickly than I had anticipated." Breathless and beaming, Mara held onto the windowsill as the duke's barouche carriage—the same one that had ferried them around Hyde Park—rolled away from the church to a flurry of well wishes and rice. They were bound for Grosvenor Square, where the festivities would continue with a seven-course dinner and dancing. But for the next twenty minutes (or however long it took the driver to navigate the crowded city streets), the newly wed couple had each other to themselves.

"How long did you think it would take?" Ambrose asked, shooting her a wry glance under the brim of his wool-felt top hat before removing the accessory and placing it on the seat.

"Hours. Days. Weeks." The corners of Mara's smile drooped slightly when she noted the strategic placement of Ambrose's hat. It rose between them like a small black hill . . . or a wall. "But it's over. It's done. We're *married*."

"So we are," he agreed, and was that a flash of displeasure in his gaze?

No, she told herself.

Surely not.

Ambrose had wanted to marry her. He'd proposed, hadn't he? Not at the gardens, but two days later, while they were on a carriage ride similar to this one. He'd had the driver stop, and he'd helped her out, and then in front of a fountain with purple lilacs all around, he'd gone down on bended knee and asked her to be his wife. She'd accepted—of course she'd accepted—and immediately found herself consumed with wedding preparations. Or rather, Kitty and the Duchess of Southwick (*Dowager Duchess,* she amended silently) had been consumed, and she'd toddled along for the ride, a bit like a child being coaxed to bed with the promise of a new story.

Occasionally, she'd wondered where Ambrose was.

More specifically, why he *wasn't* with her.

But weddings were women's business, so she hadn't worried overmuch. They'd have all the time in the world to spend together after they were married. Except now she had a ring on her finger—gold, with a diamond-shaped sapphire—and Ambrose's hat was closer to her than he was.

"Are you looking forward to the ball?" she asked, and her smile disappeared altogether when he gave a curt shake of his head.

"No, not really. I've always found them to be tedious."

But we met at a ball, she wanted to say. Except she didn't, because it wasn't *this* Ambrose that she'd met at the Glendale Ball. This was a cool, distant, slightly sardonic Ambrose who had revealed himself to her in fits and starts, but never all at once. Never like this.

Where was the man who had kissed her in the rain?

Where was the man who had shown her how to skip a rock?

Where was the man who had turned her veins to fire in the gardens?

"Ambrose, I—"

"We're here," he interrupted.

Mara struggled to pick up her smile. "So we are."

"ARE YOU FEELING all right?" Biting her lip, Mara shifted to the far side of the bed and brought the coverlet to her chin when her husband, half-dressed and holding a silver flask, staggered in from the dressing chamber. "You don't look . . . well."

"I'm fine," he grunted, hopping on his left leg while yanking his trousers off the right. Catching his balance on the ornate bedpost, he squinted blearily at her, his blue eyes bloodshot and his jaw sporting a shadow of scruff that hadn't been there this morning when they'd stood side by side in the church and committed themselves to each other before God, King, and two hundred people that Mara didn't know. "Are *you* feeling all right?"

"Nervous," she admitted softly, tightening her grip on the coverlet as if it were a layer of chainmail instead of a flimsy cotton blanket. "I'm feeling nervous."

"What is there to be nervous about?" He tipped the flask upright, drank what was left, and tossed the empty container across the room where it landed in a chair. "We've already done the difficult part."

"You mean the wedding?" she said uncertainly.

Ambrose grimaced. "Yes, the wedding. The *bloody* wedding." He raked a hand through his hair, pulling the dark ends taut. Wearing an unbuttoned shirt and nothing else, his chiseled frame was on full display in the darkened room . . . but she dared not peek below his waist.

It was too much,

This was too much.

He was too much.

"Perhaps I should sleep in my chamber for tonight." She started to swing her legs over the edge of the mattress and froze when he suddenly leapt on top of it, his knees straddling her waist and his whisky breath a whisper away from her ear.

"But this is the *enjoyable* part," he said, kissing her neck. Prying her fingers loose from the coverlet, he cast it away, baring her slender body—clothed in a singular slip of ivory satin that had felt pretty and airy in the light of day but suddenly felt far too revealing in the dead of night—to his hungry gaze. "God, you're fucking gorgeous."

"Th-thank you," she said haltingly. "Ambrose, I think—"

"Stop thinking," he growled, cupping her breasts and flicking his thumbs across her nipples in a possessive caress. Her belly jerked in response, and for a while she *did* stop thinking.

She didn't think when he nibbled a path to her ear.

She didn't think when he slid his tongue inside her mouth.

She didn't think when he stroked between her legs.

It was all a blur. A wonderful, seamless, pleasure-filled blur.

But everything came into sharp, stunning focus when she caught a glimpse of what was meant to go in her. Substantial in size, Ambrose's cock stood proudly up and away from navel, demanding attention. Wide-eyed, Mara gazed at it . . . and then immediately wished that she hadn't when her body stiffened in response.

She burrowed inward, reflexively pinching her thighs together and bringing her hands to her chest. Were the duke sober and not lost to desire, he surely would have noticed the change. But he wasn't, and he didn't.

Not until it was too late.

"Ambrose." She pushed at his shoulders, and when he didn't react, her panic grew by leaps and bounds. She used to ask her father to stop when he'd advanced toward her, malice in his eye and his fingers already curled in a meaty fist. She'd *begged* him. But it hadn't mattered. He'd hit her anyway. And now that she had that terrible image in her head, now that she'd allowed herself to remember the feeling of absolute helplessness, it was all she could think about. "Ambrose, that's enough. *I said that's enough!*"

A hand that wasn't her hand—how could it be her hand, she'd never hit anyone before—reared back and then came rushing forward, palm extended, to deliver a painful smack to the side of his cheek as he fumbled with the silk ties on her night-dress.

Caught off guard, Ambrose fell off the side of the bed and landed in a heap of blankets and bruised ego on the floor.

"I'm sorry," she gasped, scrambling onto her stomach and extending her arm. The same arm she'd just used to strike her own husband. "I didn't mean—"

"I'm fine," he snapped, brushing her hand aside as he rose unsteadily to his feet.

"But you just—"

"*I said that I'm fine, Mara.* And this . . ." His gaze hardened as it swept across the mattress. "This is finished." Finding and yanking on his trousers (backward, but she wasn't about to correct him), he left his own bedchamber, slamming the door in his wake.

"MIGHT WE HAVE a moment to speak?" Stepping nervously into her husband's study, Mara kept her eyes on the crackling fire in the hearth and away from the man sitting silently behind an enormous mahogany desk. "Mr. Humphrey said that you were available."

"Did he," Ambrose murmured, his flat tone giving her no indication of what emotions swirled behind his blank countenance. Outside, heavy sheets of rain fell from a gray, moody sky. But the dour weather was practically a tropical paradise when compared to the temperature in the study. Despite the hearty fire, a noticeable chill had settled in the air the instant Mara had entered the masculine sanctuary, causing her tongue to stick to the roof of her mouth and gooseflesh to prickle across her arms. "It appears I'll need to have a word with my butler on his definition of 'available.'"

"Don't be cross with him." At last, she dared to look at Ambrose, and her heart sank at what she saw sitting behind the desk.

Or rather, *whom* she saw.

A stranger.

A stranger in somber black, with piercing blue eyes that stood out in stark contrast from a curtain of gloomy shadow. He put down the quill pen he'd been writing with when she'd entered and rested his elbows on the desk, his gaze cool and unwavering above interlocked fingers.

"How can I help you, Mara?"

How can I help you, Mara. Hardly the words a brand-new bride wanted to hear. Not from her husband, at any rate.

Surely he was meant to give her a compliment (how fetching you look in the morning), or tell her how much he'd missed her (how I've missed you), or how in love with her he was (you're the stars to my moon). Instead, all she'd received was a brusque, detached, businesslike query. She was fairly certain her maid had asked her exactly the same thing an hour ago.

"I . . . I wanted to talk," she began. "About last night."

A muscle ticked in Ambrose's jaw. "What about last night?"

"It . . ." *Was terrible. Awful. Calamitous.* "It did not go as anticipated. I wanted to apologize. For . . . for striking you. It wasn't my intention."

"You're forgiven. If there's nothing else—"

"We can try again," she blurted.

She could tell that she'd caught him off guard by the lift of his brows.

Good, she thought, a little viciously. She wanted him off guard. She wanted him as far away from this cool, composed statue of granite as she could get.

"That won't be possible." He leaned back in his chair and crossed his legs; a deliberate attempt to intimidate that he'd likely used on dozens of opponents. But she wasn't an opponent. She was his *wife*. Why couldn't he see that?

"Why not?" she asked, summoning every ounce of courage in her possession. It wasn't an easy thing under the best of circumstances to question Ambrose, and these were hardly the best of circumstances. Come to think of it, she was hard pressed to imagine worse circumstances than a wedding night that had ended with the groom on the floor and the bride still a virgin.

"Because you're leaving. Today. For Southwick Castle."

"Leaving?" Now it was her brows that rose. "Today? No, that's not right. We'd planned to remain here, in London, for our honeymoon."

They'd already discussed it. She had a list written down of all the things they were going to do. Another visit to Kensington Gardens, a boat ride on the Serpentine, a private tour of the Royal Menagerie.

"Plans have changed."

"But . . . but I have a list," she said stupidly.

"And I have work to do. I'll call on you when it's finished."

Her lips parted in dismay. "You're not coming with me?"

"No, Mara. I am not going with you."

She considered begging, but she had pride left. Not much, but enough to graciously nod, and curtsy, and walk out of the study and all the way up to her room before she burst into tears.

CHAPTER FOURTEEN

March 1813
Southwick Castle, Derbyshire, England

"Y E HAVE TAE rest, Your Grace."

Mara flinched when Agnes placed a gentle hand on her shoulder. "Not until he wakes up."

"That might not be for another hour, or another day, or even another week."

"Then I'll wait for as long as it takes." Lifting her head—her neck was beyond numb—she squinted blearily out the window. "What time is it?"

What day is it?

Three had passed, that she knew of. Three days since the wild dogs had attacked, and she'd fended them off, and Ambrose had slipped into what the doctor was calling a "blood loss coma." With nothing else to do and nowhere else to go (how laughable, that she'd once imagined trotting off to London sans her husband when now she couldn't fathom leaving his side), she had begun to track the minutes by the steady rise and fall of Ambrose's chest. That movement, slight as it was, remained one of the few things that gave her hope.

As long as the duke breathed, he lived.

And as long as he lived, there was no reason he wouldn't soon wake up.

"Noon on the hour, Your Grace, and ye have not eaten a bite since yesterday morning." Agnes clucked her tongue in sympathetic disapproval. "I've a hot bath in your room, along with a platter of fruit and cheese. All of yer favorites. Come wash yourself and eat."

Mara sighed. "Agnes—"

"Ye can do it quickly," the Scotswoman said with the same unequivocal firmness she used to boss the other servants about. "But ye need tae do it. Come on, then. I'll stand guard over him."

"And tell me if anything changes," Mara ordered as she wearily pushed herself to her feet. "Even something small, like a movement of his finger. The doctor said that would be a sign of a progress."

"Even something small," Agnes agreed before she nudged the exhausted duchess out the door and closed it behind her.

ONCE MARA HAD departed, Agnes abruptly turned to the duke, crossed her arms, and scowled. "That's enough now, Your Grace. Ye have given us all a good scare, but it's time tae wake up. We both know ye have been through worse than this. If that monstrosity of a father couldn't defeat ye, then what chance does an inbred spaniel have?" She waited, breath bated, for the duke to open his eyes. *No one* ignored a direct command from the likes of Agnes MacCallum, and this was the first time she'd been alone with the duke to give it. The duchess, bless her heart, had left his bedside for nary a second. If it weren't under such dire circumstances, it would have warmed her heart to witness such devotion between two people who had caused each other such pain.

"Your lady is waiting for ye," she said, squeezing the duke's hand. "Dinna disappoint her, Your Grace. Ye have done enough of that already."

"YOU LOOK TERRIBLE." Kitty was there to greet her sister when Mara entered her bedchamber, although the salutation was less than complimentary. "And your hair looks like a nest for squirrels."

"Not today, Kitty." Mara's muscles, stiff from sitting in the same position for hours on end, screamed in protest when she undressed, and she all but wept with relief when she stepped into the bath that Agnes had prepared for her. Filled with bubbles, it smelled of lavender, and she closed her eyes as let her head fall back onto the curved lip of the claw foot tub and the warm water lapped up to her chin. "I'm too tired to argue with you today."

"Who said that I was arguing?" Kitty's skirts swished with indignation as she settled herself on a chair beside the tub. "I was merely making an observation."

"An unkind and unnecessary observation." Mara opened one eye. "Perhaps you should return to London. Try to make amends with your own husband instead of criticizing my appearance after I've been looking after mine."

It was a cold day in hell that Mara *ever* stood up to Kitty, let alone put her in her place. But the last few days of standing helplessly beside Ambrose as he'd teetered between life and death had hardened her. It had also shown her that there was no time for enduring petty insults and making herself small so that others—including her own sister—could feel bigger.

Kitty had grown up in the same household with the same father. She'd endured the same abuse, even though Mara had done her best to take the brunt of it. But they weren't those children any longer. They hadn't been those children in years. And they could either continue to play the same roles as they always had or they could create new ones. Better ones. Stronger ones.

Mara wasn't the poor, battered daughter of a viscount.

She was the *Duchess of Southwick*.

And it was past time that she acted like it.

"You're throwing me out?" Kitty's mouth opened to form a perfect *o* of exaggerated dismay. "After all I've done to help you?"

"What have you done?" Mara asked evenly. "Besides berate me, mock me, and question my decisions? I love you, Katherine. You are my sister. But that does not give you leave to treat me as you do."

A flicker of unreadable emotion, and then Kitty's beautiful countenance contorted into an ugly sneer. "I don't have to stay here and listen to this. Do you know why I came to this godforsaken castle? Because no one else would, not even your own husband! I am the only one who has been there for you, despite you not being there for me when I needed you most!"

"When you needed me most?" Mara's brow creased as she tried to remember an instance that she *hadn't* stepped in and taken a blow meant for her smaller sister. She hadn't caught all of them. Sometimes, when their father's fists had rained down like hammers, it had been all she could do to save herself. But she'd tried. She'd always tried, often at the expense of herself. "I don't know what you're talking about."

"No," Kitty said shrilly, "you *don't* know. Because you left to marry a duke! You left me, and what do you think he did when you were gone? Why do you think I got married so quickly, and to an *earl?*"

Water splashed over the sides of the tub as Mara sat up. "I thought you loved William. I had no idea—"

"You're right, you didn't, because you weren't there." Twin blotches of red appeared high on Kitty's cheekbones. "I'm glad that you got out. I am. I'm even glad that you're a duchess, although *you* don't seem to be. But that is the extent of my *gladness*. Love? Love has never had *anything* to do with my marriage. Goodbye, Mara. I hope that Ambrose recovers. But when he does, I won't be here to see it."

She bolted from the room, leaving Mara stunned and speech-less in water that had already started to turn cold. Summoning a maid, she remained quiet as she donned fresh clothes including a blue dress with white trim at the elevated waistline and sleeves that extended to the elbow. A comb worked out the worst of the tangles from her hair before she had the maid plait it down the middle of her back. A few bites of meat and cheese, as much to appease Agnes as to fill her own stomach, and she returned promptly to Ambrose's bedchamber.

"Has there been any change?" she asked quietly.

"No, Your Grace." Agnes shook her head. "No change."

The drapes were drawn, giving the illusion that the duke was merely taking a mid-afternoon nap as opposed to being lost to the sleep of the dead. When Mara touched his arm, his skin was cool, and she nodded at the hearth where the logs had dwindled to deep red pieces of charred wood.

"A bigger fire, please. Then you can leave us."

"Your Grace," Agnes began, her expression troubled, but Mara deliberately turned her head away.

"I'd like to be alone with my husband."

". . . yes, Your Grace."

AMBROSE WAS HAVING the most decadent dream.

It was late at night, the moon a ghostly circle in an otherwise dark and clear sky. He was in his room, sleeping, when a scent woke him.

Lilacs.

The air smelled of lilacs.

Shadows parted from his path as he strode, clothed in only a pair of loose-fitting trousers, through the blue room and into his wife's private chamber. She slept on her side with her hands pressed together beneath her cheek and her curls a tumble of red across a white pillowcase, the very picture of angelic beauty.

He must have made a sound, some creak of a floorboard, because her eyes suddenly opened. She stared at him, and he waited for her rebuke, but it never came. Instead, she propped up on her elbow, sending the thin blanket she wore slithering to her waist . . . revealing naked breasts with dusky-tipped nipples all but begging for his touch.

"Ambrose," she said, her voice husky from sleep. "I was waiting for you."

He was hard as a pike before he reached her, the top of his cock straining against the waistband of his trousers. She took him in a firm grasp when he mounted her, running her hand along the pulsing length of his erection, and on a groan he kissed her, his tongue finding a familiar home inside of her sweet, sweet mouth.

Kicking the blanket aside, he worked his lips down her body, the heels of his hands pressing firmly on her hips when she tried to arch off the mattress. "Mine," he growled possessively, laying claim to her slick curls and small pearl hidden amidst them.

Nails raked at his shoulders as he tasted her, licked her, nibbled her. As he drove her right to the edge and then yanked her ruthlessly back, drawing out her passion into an endless stream of highs and lows and *almosts*.

"Ambrose. Ambrose, p-please."

Only when she begged, only when her head thrashed, only when her eyes glazed over, did he grant her the mercy of relenting. Spreading her wet desire onto his fingers, he coated himself with it, indulging in a hard, fast pump from base to tip that nearly had him coming into his own palm.

Rolling her onto her side, he positioned himself behind her, his arm reaching around her waist to hold her snugly against the crook of his loins. "Bend your leg, love. Yes," he groaned, his jaw clenching when the new angle allowed his cock to slowly slide into her tight, velvety quim. "Yes, just like that."

He cupped her breast as he drove into her, then fanned his fingers between her legs and teased her clitoris as he withdrew. Fire ignited in his belly when she rubbed her bottom against him and he filled her again, hard and fast and deep.

Mine.

Mine.

MINE.

Their hips moved in unison, gliding back and forth, back and forth. Dancing on that razor sharp line of passion and pleasure. Gliding between darkness and desire. Grasping her chin, he turned her head toward him and captured her lips in a bruising kiss while simultaneously plunging all of him into all of her.

They came together, Ambrose with a primal snarl and Mara on a soft cry. Shuddering, he emptied his seed, again and again, until he was spent, body, mind, and soul. Keeping an arm wrapped around her ribcage, he withdrew and buried his face into her nape, breathing in the scent of her. The scent of the lilacs. The scent of complete and utter fulfillment.

Even in the hazy swirl of a dream, he recognized that with Mara, intimacy was different. It was not a means to an end, but a *belonging*. A union that he'd never experienced before with any of his previous, meaningless dalliances. And what a fool he was, to have waited this long. To have wasted untold nights.

"Mara." He kissed the delicate bump of her vertebrae. "Mara, I . . ." A bead of sweat pooled at his hairline and rolled down his temple. Annoyed, he brushed it away, but a second took its place and then a third, a fourth, a fifth. All at once, the air was swelteringly hot.

"What the devil? Mara? Mara—"

But his arms were empty.

She was gone.

Vanished.

Flames, hot and hungry, ran up the drapes and then spread across the ceiling in a crackling inferno of orange and red. Cursing, Ambrose tried to jump off the bed, but his legs wouldn't move. Neither would his arms. He was trapped, and when he tried to shout, no sound emerged. Horrified, he could only watch as the room burned.

THE NEXT MORNING, Mara woke in a chair beside Ambrose. And as soon as she absently pressed the back of her hand to his forehead and felt the heat radiating from his skull, she knew immediately that something was wrong.

"Agnes? Agnes! Come here. Come quickly!

"What is it, Your G-Grace?" Out of breath from racing up the stairs when she'd heard her mistress call out, Agnes rushed to the duke's bedside and placed her hand right above Mara's. What she felt made the blood drain from her cheeks, and in that instant Mara knew that something was very, very wrong indeed.

"What's happening to him?" she whispered, as if by keeping her voice low it would somehow keep the evils that were plaguing Ambrose at bay.

"Infection," Agnes said matter-of-factly. Rolling up her sleeves, she went to the wash basin where the doctor had ordered fresh water, clean towels, and a bar of olive oil soap to remain. "We'll have tae push him back onto his side and clean the wound. He's not going tae like it." She summoned Mr. Humphrey and Lucy, a scullery maid, who hung nervously in the doorway until Agnes barked at her to come forward and hold the towels.

"What can I do?" Mara asked, wringing her hands together.

"Stay by his head. Keep him still."

Keep him still?

He hadn't moved in days.

Nonetheless, Mara did what was requested of her. If Agnes had told her to stand on her head and cluck like a chicken she would have done that, too. Anything to make Ambrose feel better. To wake him up. To return him to the robust health he'd once known.

I don't even care if you're cantankerous and terrible to deal with, she thought as she tentatively placed her hands on his shoulders. *I'd rather have you like that than not have you at all.*

From the foot of the bed, she heard Agnes expel a hiss of breath.

"What?" she said anxiously. "What is it?"

"Best not tae look, Your Grace."

"He's *my* husband. If there's anything . . . oh." Dizziness hit her like a wave as her eyes went to the wound on his leg where green and yellow puss oozed. With the bandages removed, the smell was nearly overwhelming. As her stomach rolled, she yanked her gaze away. "Oh, how did we miss that? I checked it just yesterday!"

"Infection can set in overnight," Agnes said grimly. "Best ye noticed his fever when ye did, or else it would have continued tae fester. I'll clean it as best we can and send for the doctor again. We'll give him some laudanum for the pain and then hope for the best."

"Hope for the best," Mara repeated in a strangled voice as she looked at her husband. "*Hope for the best.* All we've done is hope for the best! There has to be more that we can do. A remedy we haven't tried. A medicine that would heal him!"

Agnes exchanged a fleeting glance with Mr. Humphrey.

"What?" Mara demanded. "What is it?"

"There is a doctor I've heard about in London." Another fleeting glance. "A woman."

"A *woman* doctor?" she said, amazed.

"Aye. She's supposed tae be an expert in diseases of the flesh. Except she doesn't travel. Refuses tae. I dinna know if she'll come here—"

"She will," Mara said, speaking with newfound determination. "I'll get her myself. She can't refuse me, I'm the Duchess of Southwick."

"Yes," Agnes murmured, pride warring with distress as her heart was pulled in opposite directions. To the duke she'd loved since he was a boy. And to the duchess that she'd had the honor of watching turn from a shy, awkward duckling into an elegant, powerful swan. "Yes, ye certainly are, lass. Ye certainly are."

CHAPTER FIFTEEN

MARA DIDN'T WANT to leave Ambrose, but as her carriage raced off to London, at least she was content with the knowledge that she was doing *something* to save him. Something other than sitting around and waiting for the worst to happen.

Drumming her fingers on the windowsill, she silently urged the driver to go faster. Derbyshire to London, a journey of more than 150 miles, would take the rest of the day and half the night. An outrider had already been sent ahead to share the news of her impending arrival with the staff at Mill House, after which he was to report directly to the private residence of one Dr. Abigail Chadwick and deliver the letter that Mara had hastily dashed together. A letter that she prayed would be enough to convince the doctor to travel back with her to Southwick Castle, but if not, she was prepared to persuade her with words. On her knees, if need be, for she wasn't afraid to beg for the man she loved.

And she *did* love him.

Ambrose.

Part of her always had. All of her always would.

No matter what happened.

Mara, I . . .

She was determined that he would have the opportunity to finish that sentence.

Somewhere around Northampton, Mara slipped into an

exhausted, dreamless sleep and did not awake until she heard a knock on the carriage door seconds before it opened, letting in a waft of cool night air that smelled of vaguely of brackish water and chimney smoke. London at its finest.

"We're here, Your Grace," a footman announced formally. "Mill House."

"What—what time is it?" She rubbed the tension at the base of her neck as she hopped down from the carriage and gazed warily at her husband's London manor. This was where she'd spent her wedding night, a memory that did not invoke over-whelming feelings of joy. She had never pictured herself coming back to this place. This stone tomb of bad beginnings. But then, neither had she pictured herself taking a lover, or standing up to her husband, or fending off a pack of stray dogs. What was life, if not a series of pictures that you painted as you went? Sometimes with more grays. Other times with vivid reds and oranges. Always changing. Always evolving. Always bringing you, canvas by canvas, to where you were truly meant to be.

If this was where her marriage had broken, then perhaps it was only right that this was where it was supposed to be fixed. Where she was meant to save the husband that had sent her away. Where she was meant to save the man who had stolen her heart.

"The hour is half past midnight, Your Grace," the footman informed her. "Should I have your belongings brought straight to your chamber?"

"I didn't bring any belongings. But I'll take a cup of tea."

She sat in the front parlor and sipped her tea by candlelight, her nerves too frayed to sleep. A hundred times over wondered if she'd made the right decision in leaving Ambrose. What sort of wife left her husband when he was hovering in that dark, gloomy place between life and death? *A wife who cares,* she told herself. *A wife who is willing to fight for her happy ending.*

Ambrose had come out to the orchards to fight for her.

Despite all his failings, he was there when she needed him

most.

He hadn't run.

He hadn't left her.

He had risked his life, and sustained a serious, life-threatening injury as a result, to save her (never mind that she'd already mostly saved herself). If there was a chance, however small, that this doctor knew how to help him . . . then she was in the right place. She had to be. Because the alternative was too terrible to even think about.

Refilling her cup, she drank her tea and waited for the sun to rise.

⋙⋘

"WHY WOULD YOU do that?" Humphrey asked in a hushed tone as he and Agnes waited outside the duke's door. They'd just finished cleaning his wound for the second time and he was resting fitfully, his fever having miraculously broken over the long night.

"Do what?" Agnes asked, busying herself with folding a pile of clean linens.

"Send the duchess away. To London, of all places!"

"I dinna *send* her away. I told her about a doctor that might be able tae assist the duke with his recovery. She chose tae go of her own accord. As for London, it can hardly be helped that that is where Dr. Chadwick resides."

"First thing, Dr. Chadwick isn't even a doctor. Not a real one. And secondly, you know what His Grace will think if he wakes while she is gone and finds that she's in *London*," Humphrey hissed, his countenance growing mottled. "You've heard the gossip, same as I."

"Indeed I have," Agnes said calmly.

"Then if he does come to before she returns, I'll make sure to promptly inform him that the duchess's travels have nothing to do with the unsubstantiated rumors of an affair. Lest the entire country believe that while the Duke of Southwick teetered at death's door, the Duchess of Southwick flitted off to London in search of—of a male paramour!"

Agnes stopped mid-fold. "Ye will do nothing of the kind."

Humphrey's chin wobbled with indignation. "But—"

"Do ye ken why rocks in a stream are smooth, Mr. Humphrey?"

"What do rocks—"

"Because the water wears them down. It doesn't happen all at once. Sometimes it takes years. But with enough gentle pressure, the hardest, roughest edges are worn smooth. That's why ye are not going tae tell His Grace anything if he wakes, other than tae share that Her Grace has gone tae London. The rest will be up tae him."

Comprehension flickered, like a candle being lit. "You started the rumors, didn't you? About the duchess. *Agnes*."

Stacking the folded towels together, she scooped them up. "*If* I happened to read something that revealed the duchess was considering taking a lover, and *if* I shared that plan with a few maids known tae have loose tongues, and *if* that gossip was the reason His Grace came home, I make no apologies."

"This—this is beyond the pale, Agnes!" Humphrey blustered. "Even for you."

The Scotswoman merely lifted a brow. "Help me with the rest of these linens, if ye please. Heaven knows where that Lucy has gone off to this time. Lazy girl. How can she ever hope tae rise above scullery maid if she isn't here when I need her tae be?"

Humphrey opened his mouth, but before he could muster a reply, a loud, hacking cough emanated from inside the duke's chambers. Startled, Agnes dropped the entire bundle of towels she'd just painstakingly folded.

"Oh my," she gasped, her hands going to her cheeks. "He's awake!"

She and Humphrey fought for who would be the first through the door. Agnes, with her wide hips, was the winner.

Blocking off the butler with a swish of her derriere, she rushed to Ambrose's bedside and dropped to her knees beside the mattress.

"Your Grace," she said earnestly. "How are ye feeling?"

WHAT DAY WAS it?

What month?

What *year*?

As Ambrose swam toward the surface of consciousness, he found himself properly disoriented. His tongue was also coated in a layer of cotton, and his leg hurt like the dickens.

Grimacing, he licked his lips and struggled into a sitting position. He could see that he was in his room at Southwick Castle and that it was early morning if the slices of yellow and orange streaming in between the partially drawn drapes were any indication. But other than that, he was left with a vague sense of obliviousness.

"You were bitten, Your Grace," said Mr. Humphrey, looking even more solemn than usual.

"On the leg," Agnes added.

"You lost a lot of blood."

"The doctor called it a blood loss coma."

"Then infection set it, and fever along with it."

That explained the dream he'd had. The vivid, sensual dream that had begun with lilacs and ended with fire. Reaching for a glass of water, Ambrose gulped it down, and when that didn't quench his thirst, picked up the entire pitcher. Swiping a hand across his mouth, he looked first at his butler, then his housekeeper, dark brows arching high in expectation. "Well, where is she? Where is my wife? Where is Mara?"

Agnes rose to her feet and, although it must have been his eyes playing tricks on him, appeared to back up and stomp directly onto Humphrey's instep. "She's gone, Your Grace."

"Gone?" he repeated, confused. "Gone where? Humphrey, what's wrong with your face? It's turning purple."

Another stomp, this one harder than the last.

What the *devil* was going on?

"If someone doesn't tell me where Mara is this instant—"

"London," Humphrey blurted. "She's in London."

London.

There was only one reason Mara would be in London. One reason she would leave Southwick Castle. One reason she would abandon him . . . as he had abandoned her.

One reason.

And it was all his bloody fault.

"I have to fix this," he rasped, an undercurrent of pain cutting through his voice as he ripped off the blanket, gave his bandaged leg a cursory glance, and then ignored it in favor of searching for clothes to wear. "I have to get to her. I have to tell her before it's too late."

"Tell her what, Your Grace?" Agnes asked softly.

"That I love her." He yanked a shirt over his head, then a waistcoat. "I have to tell her that I love her."

❯❯❯❯❯❯❮❮❮❮❮❮

THE MEETING WITH Dr. Chadwick had not gone . . . well.

After waiting—and wasting—an entire *day* for the doctor to complete her rounds in London's nefarious East End, Mara had finally been permitted an audience at half past ten the following morning. It was clear that the woman was brilliant, but it was equally obvious that she was more than a tad eccentric. For the duration of their meeting she had tapped, fidgeted, and paced around the primary room of her flat: a parlor filled top to bottom with glass jars, various instruments of measurement, dried herbs, and a rather alarming number of cats.

"Sorry," she'd said finally, after Mara had run out of ways to ask the doctor to travel back with her to Derbyshire. "I cannot

153

help you. I don't leave London, you see."

"But you have to make an exception," Mara had pleaded. "Ambrose is *dying*."

Here, Dr. Chadwick had paused and blinked, her green eyes owlishly large behind a pair of gold spectacles. "Is he dead?"

"No. That is, I don't think so. But—"

"Then he's not dying. Take this"—she'd thrust a glass jar at Mara half filled with a white, powdery substance—"and sprinkle it over the wound three times a day. Three times, do you understand? No more, no less."

"What is it?" Mara had asked, unscrewing the lid and taking a tentative sniff.

Dr. Chadwick had pursed her lips. "I don't know. I haven't given it a name yet."

"You don't *know*? But then how—"

"Good day, your duchess. Lady Duchess. Your lady. Your Grace? I can never remember how you British prefer to be addressed. Bunch of nonsense, if you ask me. But then, nobody does. You have to go now. I have to feed my cats." And then, as if Mara were a large cat herself, Dr. Chadwick had picked up a broom and shooed her out the door. "Good luck!" she'd called cheerfully. "Remember, three times a day. Don't forget."

Mara had considered refusing to leave the doorstep until the doctor reconsidered her position on travel, but she'd already been in London for more than a day and she needed to get back to Southwick Castle. She needed to get back to Ambrose. But no sooner had she entered the foyer and started to remove her gloves than she discovered *Ambrose* had already come to *her*.

"Mara. Mara. *Mara*." He limped as he ran to her, and her immediate concern was his leg.

"Ambrose! What . . . what are you doing here?" she cried when he wrapped his arms around her and simply closed her into his chest, drawing her against him like a child drawing the blankets up and over their head. "You should be in bed, resting! How did you *get* here?"

"A carriage. I had to see you. I had to stop you." He took a step back and placed his hands on her shoulders. There were blackish circles under his eyes and his skin was pale, but his blue eyes were fierce. "Don't leave me, Mara. Don't choose another man. Not when I'm standing right in front of you. I'm sorry," he said, his voice cracking. "I'm sorry it took me this long. I'm sorry that I was so bloody late. But I'm here, Mara. I'm here. I'm *here*."

"Ambrose," she said, shocked to her very core. "Ambrose, you're . . . crying?"

"Bloody dust," he cursed, turning his head to the side. Gently laying her hand on his cheek, feeling the pulse of muscle and emotions he'd always done his best to hide, she turned it back. She turned time back. She turned *them* back, to that ballroom when they first met; two broken people finding their broken pieces in each other.

"Look at me, Ambrose."

"I am," he said hoarsely.

"Tell me that you love me."

"Mara, I do. I do love you. I *have* loved you." He rested his temple against hers, his tears mingling with her own as they embraced. "I was a fool. I *am* a fool. That much won't change. But my appreciation for you and the value that I place in you will. It already has. God knows I don't deserve you, but I'm going to love you anyway. Yesterday, today, for all of our tomorrows . . . I will love you, Marabelle. When I am angry, I will love you. When I am sad, I will love you. And when I want to push you away . . . I will love you most of all."

"Is that a promise?" she whispered, standing on her toes to press a soft kiss to his damp cheek as her heart swelled to twice its normal size.

"A promise, a vow." He tenderly brushed a curl behind her ear. "A lifetime."

"Then I shall accept your vow and make one of my own. I will love you, Ambrose, when I am happy. I will love you when I am tired. And when you try to push me away . . . I will love you most of all. Because we need each other. We always have."

"We always will."

"Yes," she said, smiling through her tears. "We always will."

And in the same house where their marriage had nearly come to an end, the Duchess and Duke of Southwick turned the page to a beautiful new beginning.

EPILOGUE

Several Weeks Later
Southwick Castle

AMBROSE WOKE IN the middle of the night to find Mara missing.

As he always did these days—ever since their reconciliation in London—he reached for her before he'd even opened his eyes, searching for her warm, delectable little body to tuck in against his side. But when his arm kept reaching all the way to the far side of the mattress and there was no Mara to be found, he frowned and sat up, casting the blankets aside to pad barefoot through the blue room and into her bedchamber, a room now exclusively reserved for getting dressed.

Her frame made a long, slender silhouette under an ivory quilt. Her hair a spill of vibrant red on a plain white pillowcase. She stirred when he whispered her name, then rolled onto her side and opened one eye when he spoke it again.

"What are you doing in here?" he asked.

"You were snoring," she said before muffling a yawn. "I couldn't sleep."

"The devil I was," he said, deeply offended. "Dukes don't snore."

"This duke does." A smile peeked through her sleepiness. "Don't worry. I won't tell anyone."

"Mara," he said suddenly as a memory, real and yet not real, tickled at the corner of his subconscious. A memory of this room, and lilacs, and Mara naked in her bed. "Are you still wearing your nightdress?"

Her lovely pink blush gave her away. "I was hot."

She might have been hot, but he was already on bloody fire even before he joined her in the bed. The mattress sagged beneath his weight as he straddled her, stretching her slim arms above her head and nuzzling the sensitive space between her jaw and the curve of her neck.

"Mara, my love," he said between kisses.

"Hmmm?" she moaned, raking her fingers through his hair when he released his hold on her wrists in order to cup her breasts and lift a taut nipple to his mouth.

"I don't *really* snore, do I?"

"Like a bear."

That earned her a harmless smack on her bottom as they changed positions; her on top and him on the bottom. After that, there were no more questions for quite a while and when their lovemaking had concluded, they remained in Mara's bed, their limbs entwined and their hearts beating in unison.

"You know," she said quietly, "I never asked."

"Asked what?" he mumbled, already half asleep.

"Why you came to London that day. Your leg was practically still bleeding."

He lifted his head. "I came to London because that's where you were, and because I wasn't about to let some puny weakling of a man take *my* duchess."

"I don't think I would have ever gone through with it," she said thoughtfully, winding an arm behind her head. "The affair, that is. I never *really* wanted anyone but you."

"Good, because I never wanted anyone but you." Grinning, he shook off the dregs of slumber as another part of his body came abruptly awake once more. "In fact, I do believe I want you right now."

"Again?" she asked, her eyes widening.

"Again." And with a very bearish growl, he pounced.

IN A SIMILAR bedroom over a hundred miles away, a different married couple was having a much less . . . amicable conversation.

"What do you mean, you won't go forward with the divorce?" Kitty demanded, driving her heel into the carpeted floor as she glared at her husband.

"It's late, Katherine," William sighed, and he knew—he *knew*—that she hated it when he called her that, which only served to spike her temper higher. "Can't we get some sleep and address this in the morning?"

"We can address it *now*," she seethed.

"There will be no divorce." He gave a casually dismissive wave of his arm. "There. It's done."

A myriad of emotions swirled through Kitty's body at her husband's proclamation.

Fury.

Hopelessness.

Anguish.

"But you said—" she began before he cut her off with an impatient snarl.

"I was not being *serious*, Katherine. I spoke of divorce in a moment of anger. You know as well as I that it isn't a feasible option."

"It could be. If we petitioned the courts—"

"No," he said flatly.

"But you don't *want* to be married to me! Not when you love her."

William closed the book he'd been pretending to read with a violent snap. "I said I don't care to speak of her."

"Why not?" Kitty said shrilly. "She's always right here, whether we speak of her or not. In our house. In our carriage. In our *bed*. She's here all the time, and I for one am sick of it. I won't live like this, William. I won't have three people in this marriage when I only said vows to one."

A thundercloud rolled across the Earl of Radcliffe's countenance. When it had cleared, he raised his hand in the air and crooked his finger. "Come here, Katherine."

"I don't want to," she said, shaking her head from side to side.

"Katherine—"

"*Fine.*" Her feet dragged across the floor as she obeyed his summons. His arms shot out and he caught her around the waist, swinging her easily up and onto his lap. At first, she wanted to deny him. She *always* wanted to deny him. To resist the traitorous feelings swirling around inside of her. Feelings of lust. Of longing. Of desire. But it was a futile endeavor.

Her mind may have hated William, but her body . . .

Her body was helpless to resist him.

About the Author

Jillian Eaton grew up in Maine and now lives in Pennsylvania on a farmette with her husband and their three boys. They share the farm with a cattle dog, an old draft mule, a thoroughbred, and a mini-donkey—all rescues. When she isn't writing, Jillian enjoys spending time with her animals, gardening, reading, and going on long walks with her family.

Milton Keynes UK
Ingram Content Group UK Ltd.
UKHW011819090224
437558UK00013B/528